What the critics are saying

Reviews for *LOVE MAGIC*

"...remarkable tales that will keep you fascinated and begging for more." - *Sensual Romance*

"Love Magic is enchanting in every way!" - *Timeless Tales*

"Ann Jacobs' stories start out with steam and mellow out with what's really important - romance. Love Magic is sexy and hot enough to warm you up without a fire or a cozy blanket!" - *A Romance Review*

"Love Magic certainly sizzles with scorching sex, but it's true love that warms the heart, and makes this book worth reading." - *WordWeaving*

Reviews for *LOVE SLAVE*

"...a fun read with unexpected depth. The harem scenes were certainly HOT! I loved Bear's willingness to go to great lengths to satisfy Shana's fantasies -- and then turn their joint fantasy into reality." - *Sensual Romance*

"This is one excellent hot, steamy read." - *Sensual Romance*

"...despite its short length, you get to know Shana and Bear, and are pulled into their sensuous fantasy romance. Highly recommended." - *WordWeaving*

Discover for yourself why readers can't get enough of the multiple-award-winning publisher Ellora's Cave. Whether you prefer e-books or paperbacks, be sure to visit EC on the web at www.ellorascave.com for an erotic reading experience that will leave you breathless.

www.ellorascave.com

Ellora's Cave Publishing, Inc.
PO Box 787
Hudson, OH 44236-0787

ISBN # 1843605546

A Mutual Favor, edited by Allie Sawyer.
Cover art by Scott Carpenter.

Warning: The following material contains strong sexual
content meant for mature readers. *A Mutual Favor* has been
rated Hard R, erotic, by a minimum of three independent
reviewers. We strongly suggest storing this book in a place
where young readers not meant to view it are unlikely to
happen upon it. That said, enjoy…

A MUTUAL FAVOR

Written by

ANN JACOBS

Chapter One

Hearing about his ex-wife's latest legal salvo topped off what had already been a disaster of a day.

Doctor Kurt Silverman shed his lab coat and sat for the first time since six o'clock this morning. Eyes closed, he leaned back in his desk chair and tried to clear his mind.

"Hey, Silverman, it's after hours. Couldn't you sleep better at home?"

Kurt opened one eye at the familiar sound of Shelly Ware's voice. "Shel. What's up?"

"Not much. I just finished Brad Gale's therapy. He has trouble getting here during regular hours."

Kurt recalled a fifty-ish financial analyst whose knee he'd repaired two months ago. "It's nice of you to stay late so he doesn't miss his rehab."

"I try to accommodate him when I can. His boss isn't very flexible about his working hours. I saw your light on and decided to come say hello on my way out."

She frowned. "What's wrong? You look as though you just lost your best friend."

"I'm okay. Long day, lots of problems."

"Want to unload some of them?"

Kurt shrugged, then grimaced at the pain that followed his sudden movement. "A rubdown would do me more good."

"Swivel that chair around and I'll see what I can do."

She laid her hands on his shoulders and began to knead, softly at first, then harder. Kurt closed his eyes and shut down his mind to everything except her touch, and the not-unpleasant smell of deep-heating rub that he associated with his pal Shelly.

The furnace blower kicked in, its sound a throaty, relaxing sort of purr. Shelly paused, as if distracted by the noise.

"Don't stop. Did anybody ever tell you you've got a magic touch?"

She laughed. "Nobody but you. You're the surgeon with the magic hands. I'm just an overworked, underpaid physical therapist. By the way, Mrs. Anderson was moving her leg better today."

"Thanks. Any good news is welcome on a day like this. Adrianna's pet shark has trumped up new excuses to drag me back into court. I swear the woman won't quit punishing me until I'm dead and she's picked my bones clean."

"Is there anything I can do to make things better?"

Kurt shrugged. "Not unless you know a hit man who specializes in ex-wives." He picked up the correspondence from his lawyer, then slapped it back onto the desk. "She wants to restrict my visits with Jason."

"Kurt, no!" Shelly resumed massaging his shoulders, her touch fiercer than before.

"Unfortunately, yes."

"Why?"

"I live in a pigsty, work all the time, and ignore my son when he's here. According to Adrianna, that is."

Kurt's muscles tightened, but Shelly soon had the knots worked out. When she stepped away, her warmth stayed with him.

Unshed tears made her eyes sparkle in the fluorescent glow from the ceiling lights. "I'm so sorry."

"Me, too. Sorry I married Adrianna. Hell, I wish I'd joined a monastery before I met her."

A grin lurked at the corners of her mouth. "Kurt, you're not even Catholic."

"I should have converted."

"And disappointed all the moms who had hopes of marrying their daughters off to Dr. Silverman?" Now a smile lit up her whole face.

Kurt returned her grin.

He couldn't stay depressed too long around Shelly. Unlike most women, she didn't set his defenses on alert. Besides, she had a way of making life's problems seem less pressing.

"Don't mind me. I'll survive somehow. Are we still on for Friday night to celebrate you growing another year older?"

"Just try to weasel out." She shot a playful look his way. "I'm assuming you won't get too decrepit by then to hoist your margarita."

He chuckled. "I'll manage. Hey, if you're not doing anything tonight, why don't we go over to your place? I'll spring for pizza with the works if you've got a couple of cold beers."

"Sorry. I have plans."

"Hot date?"

Kurt kept smiling, though the thought of his good pal Shelly getting tangled in the sheets with some sex-starved resident made him want to find the guy and strangle him.

A voice inside his head reminded him Shelly's sex life wasn't his concern. That who and when she fucked was none of his damn business.

As if she thought his question was a joke, she laughed. "Hardly a hot date. I told my sister and brother-in-law I'd entertain their kids so they can have a little time to themselves." She glanced at her watch. "Oh, no. They're going to drop Gretchen and Tommy at my apartment in half an hour. I've got to get a move on."

"Go, then. Hey, thanks for stopping by. You're better at lifting my spirits than a fistful of psych meds."

"Really? Pity I can't bottle myself up and sell me. Hey, chin up. Everything will come out okay. No judge in his right mind will say Jason shouldn't spend time with you."

With that, Shelly stood and brushed her lips across Kurt's cheek. Then, as suddenly as she'd appeared, she walked out.

A few minutes later, he left the building. A gust of cold wind chafed his skin and tousled his hair as he crossed the courtyard in front of the hospital.

When he opened the door to his apartment, silence greeted him. Silence and the tick-tock of the alarm clock on the floor beside his bed.

Kurt wished he weren't alone.

He'd really wanted Shelly's company tonight. He told himself he needed her to keep his mind off Adrianna and the new custody war she'd just declared.

* * * * *

Shelly choked back tears as she tucked Tommy and Gretchen into bed. She was still reeling with shock from her sister's news.

Damn it. It wasn't fair.

Donna was only a year older than she, with years of living to look forward to. She had a husband who loved her and these two precious kids.

She couldn't have cancer.

But she did. In two days, Donna would check into the hospital for a hysterectomy.

They caught it early. I'll be okay.

Donna had sounded brave, but Shelly imagined she was scared to death. Shelly was terrified, not only for her sister but for herself.

The same thing might happen to her. Fate might shut off her biological clock before its time.

She'd recently begun to hear that clock's gentle ticking in her head. Now it sounded like a metronome gone berserk.

Suddenly dizzy, Shelly bent and kissed the children. Then she stumbled out of the small guest room. Tears streamed from her eyes.

She wanted kids. At least one, maybe more. Suddenly she felt compelled to begin having them. Now.

She laughed through her tears. This was one compulsion she couldn't act out on her own, and she had no hot daddy prospect in mind.

Hot? Ha! She had no daddy prospect, hot or cold.

It was her own fault for being so particular. She shouldn't have blown off perfectly acceptable marriage candidates who'd done nothing wrong except for failing to set off the bells she foolishly expected to hear when she found Mr. Right.

She'd heard those bells. Recognized the symptoms they set off inside her. Unfortunately those bells had been ringing for two years, for one man. As unlikely a lover as she could have found if she'd gone out looking.

She had lost her head and hormones to a man who was terminally over love. He put out warning signals as loud as fire alarms to any woman who tried to breach the walls around his heart. If he ever thought about her as a woman and not a pal, he'd run away from her as fast as he could.

Kurt Silverman was the epitome of Mr. Wrong.

Damn him anyway. Damn his silky dark hair and his brooding, slate-gray eyes. Curse the killer smile that drew women like honey drew flies.

To hell with the gorgeous doctor and the chip his ex-wife had left on his shoulder as a souvenir of their marriage.

Part of Shelly wished she'd never met him.

Why had Kurt come to San Antonio to lick his wounds following a bitter divorce? And why had he joined the trauma surgery practice where she worked as a rehabilitative services specialist?

Worse, why had she not kept her distance? She'd known from the start that the man sported raw emotional scars.

Her getting the hots for Doctor Silverman had been a nasty twist of fate.

Not as nasty a twist as Donna getting cancer, of course. And she had no business mooning over Kurt or worrying about her own future when her thoughts should have been on her sister.

As she sat on the couch and stared at the blank TV screen, though, Shelly couldn't help trying to recall what kinds of cancer ran in families.

Cervical cancer? She didn't think so, but couldn't recall for sure. But she figured that if she wanted to hold her own babies in her arms, it was past time for her to get busy having them.

An icy wave of fear washed over her.

That metronome inside her head ticked away, sending shards of pain to her temples.

She got up and took two ibuprofen tablets before stumbling off to bed. When the throbbing subsided, she scolded herself for worrying about her own trivial problems when it was Donna who deserved her concern.

* * * * *

"We can postpone celebrating if you want," Kurt said on Friday when Shelly mentioned that her sister had come out of surgery an hour earlier.

Shelly shook her head. His concern warmed her, but there was nothing she could do for Donna now. She'd sleep away the day and night, mercifully sedated.

"Not on your life. I'm going to need that margarita."

"Me, too." When he grinned, fine lines accentuated his eyes. "Scrubs?"

They did their celebrating in OR garb. Shelly recalled the start of that tradition and their friendship almost two years ago, when they had run into each other outside surgery and decided to grab a bite together at a restaurant on the nearby Riverwalk.

"Scrubs it is. Seven o'clock?"

"Let's make it six. I'm finished in surgery for the day, barring any major emergencies. Unless that's too early."

"No. Six is fine."

"Good. What sort of memento would you like to mark the passing of yet another year?"

Shelly didn't know. She'd given Kurt a floppy-eared basset hound stuffed toy not long ago when he turned thirty-six because he'd made a passing comment that he'd like someday to have a pet, and last week he'd brought her a huge scarlet teddy bear toting a pound of Valentine candy. She'd had to keep reminding herself the card around Teddy's neck read "To my good pal Shelly"…not "To My Valentine".

"Surprise me with another pet for my menagerie." Suddenly an idea surfaced. "On second thought, I'd like to ask a very special favor."

"Name it. It's yours."

She smiled, but her stomach felt as if she'd tied it up in knots. "Don't make promises unless you know what it is that you're agreeing to. I'll tell you what I want, tonight."

That is, she'd tell him if she didn't come to her senses before then.

"Okay." He glanced at the clock on the wall and shrugged. "I have to run. Patients will be stacked up in the waiting room three deep if I don't get a move on. If you're doing Mrs. Anderson's therapy, tell her I'll come in and check her progress tomorrow."

"Okay. 'Bye."

She shooed him down the hall, then watched until he grabbed a patient chart from its holder and disappeared into one of the examining rooms.

Later that day, between patients, Shelly leaned back in her desk chair, closed her eyes and let her imagination transport her. What if Kurt said yes?

What if…What would his hands feel like on her naked skin? He'd be gentle, caring—of that much she was certain. His beard stubble would tickle her neck…her breasts.

He'd take his time, arouse her. Then…they'd make love and nine months later she'd have a dark-haired, silvery-eyed miniature of him.

"You've got it bad, don't you?"

Oh, no. She'd been caught fantasizing again, by none other than Lynn Blackstone, one of the other physical therapists who worked for the group practice—and the wife of one of the doctors.

"Morning, Lynn," she said when she turned and met the other woman's knowing gaze.

"Good morning, yourself. How did your sister's surgery go?"

"Smoothly. I thought I'd come on in to work. Sitting by Donna's bed and watching her sleep wasn't doing her much good."

"I'm glad you're here. Dale didn't show up again this morning, so we're shorthanded." Lynn smiled. "When are you going to admit you'd like to check out what's inside Kurt's pants?"

"Never. Forget trying to make us into a couple. It won't be all that long before you can practice matchmaking on little Beth." Shelly didn't envy the Blackstones' toddler, though with luck her mother's penchant for promoting romance would mellow over the next fifteen or twenty years.

"Kurt and I are just good friends," she told Lynn for what must have been the hundredth time.

"Kurt Silverman has your pussy tied up in knots. And he likes you, which is more than he's let himself feel for any other woman since he's been here. You ought to make a move on him. Seduce him. It's no fun living like a nun, and you're not getting any younger."

"Gee, thanks. See you later," Shelly said as she tried to make her escape.

Lynn placed a hand on Shelly's shoulder. "Anytime. By the way, happy birthday."

* * * * *

A few hours later Shelly was sitting across a table from Kurt at her favorite Mexican restaurant adjacent to San Antonio's historic marketplace, the Mercado.

Diners at nearby tables might have believed they were lovers, if they'd been watching when Kurt lifted an errant curl off her forehead or stroked her hand when the waiter took their order.

The strolling guitarist had obviously assumed they were more than friends when he hit Kurt up for a tip to play a favorite song. He might easily have thought the cloisonné basset hound charm Kurt fastened around her neck signified more than friendship.

People might even have assumed the breathtakingly handsome guy in green surgical scrubs planned to take her home after dinner and make love all night long.

But they'd be wrong. She and Kurt were good friends. Nothing more. He had no more interest in her pussy than he would in a real live cat. She had to remember that.

"Thanks for the 'hush puppy,'" she said, holding the little charm away from her chest so she could look at it. "I love him."

He poured the last of the frozen margaritas from a liter beaker. "I thought you'd like him. Just how old are you now? Thirty-one or thirty-two?"

"Thirty-two."

Mariachis tapped out a rhythmic cadence in the background. Shelly and Kurt sipped their drinks and chatted about hospital politics, mutual patients, shared friends.

The sounds of mournful Spanish melodies and mellow harmonies from acoustic guitars muted but couldn't quite silence the ticking clock inside Shelly's head.

The waiter brought quesadillas oozing cheese and peppers, garnished with mild, tongue-soothing guacamole. After they'd polished off the appetizers, he set gazpacho and sizzling steak fajitas before them. Tex-Mex favorites Kurt had developed a taste for since coming to San Antonio. Dishes Shelly had loved all her life.

"Hey, what can I say? We're compatible," Kurt commented after they agreed the restaurant's dessert specialty, vanilla ice cream balls rolled in toasted coconut, couldn't hold a candle to plain old caramel flan.

"Sure we are."

Shelly only wished.

When Kurt squeezed her hand, shards of sexual awareness streaked up her arm. Apparently he felt nothing, or if he did, the heat didn't affect him the way it did her.

After the waiter set down their desserts, Kurt took Shelly's hand. "Come on. I've been waiting eight hours to find out. What is this favor you want?"

"A baby."

Oh, God. She'd done it now.

When she tried to laugh as though her wish were a joke, she found she'd suddenly gone mute.

Someone should have caught Kurt's look on film, because his expression was a perfect rendition of shocked disbelief.

"You want what?"

"A baby."

"Then by all means, have one. But why tell me?"

Shelly drew in a deep breath, then made herself look him in the eye. "Because I want you …to…"

Get me pregnant? Knock me up? She couldn't say that.

And she couldn't look at him.

Her mouth felt dry. She couldn't breathe. Couldn't swallow. Finally she focused her gaze on the untouched flan that quivered on his plate.

"I want you to donate the sperm," she blurted out before she could tear back the words.

Kurt couldn't have been more shocked if Shelly had asked him to commit murder.

Had anyone else heard her? He shot a surreptitious glance around the immediate area but noticed no outraged stares directed their way.

His cheeks burned. "You've got to be kidding," he whispered in the hope that they could keep this strictly between them.

"I wasn't." She sounded as though he'd kicked her dog, which made him feel about six inches high.

It also made him want to strike out at her. "Then you must be crazy. Flat out insane."

Unfortunately that comment came out of his mouth loud enough to draw some outside attention.

From the mortified look on her face, he guessed she noticed that folks had begun to stare.

"Kurt, forget it. Forget I said anything." Tears glistened in her eyes, but she blinked them away.

Before he could say more, she pushed her flan aside, got up, and headed for the nearest exit.

"Damn it." Kurt tossed some money on the table, grabbed their coats, and took off after her.

Chapter Two

There she was on a concrete bench in the courtyard, shivering and crying her eyes out. She didn't seem to notice the cool breeze that had kicked up since they went inside the restaurant.

Kurt had almost forgotten how much he hated seeing a woman bawl. Seeing Shelly like this refreshed his memory of how Adrianna had used tears to put a positive twist on whatever transgression he'd caught her in at any time.

Shelly wasn't like his bitch ex-wife, though. She was his pal. And pals didn't make each other cry.

He sat and threaded her arms into her coat, then drew her head onto his shoulder. "Shall we start this discussion over? Look, I'm sorry I called you crazy. You're the sanest person I know. But Shel, you couldn't have shocked me more if you'd poked me with a cattle prod."

She sniffed a few times before the tears stopped falling. "Sorry. Like I said before, forget I asked. It was a dumb idea. I—"

"Don't apologize. Hell, I'm flattered that you asked me. Not that I'd do it. And not that I don't still think it's a lousy idea for a single woman to want to take on the responsibility for a kid.

"Tell me, what brought on this sudden need to procreate?"

"My sister."

Suddenly Kurt understood. Shelly's sister having had a hysterectomy must have scared her maternal instincts into high gear.

"So, let's see if I've got this right. All of a sudden you can't wait to be a mom until you come across the guy who makes you think about forever kind of promises?"

"I may not have that kind of time."

Shelly sounded strained when she confessed her sister's surgery had made her think seriously that she might not have much time left to start a family of her own.

"I'm not a very nice person. I should be worrying about Donna, not about whether I'll ever get to hold my own baby in my arms."

He ran his hand up and down her back, felt her tension. "You'll meet the right guy and have his babies. What man in his right mind could resist you?"

"Apparently you have no trouble withstanding my charms." She laughed, a soft, sad sound that made him feel even more like a worm. "Does that make you crazy?"

"Come on, cut me some slack here. We're pals. Why would I risk losing my best friend just to grab a few hours' pleasure between the sheets?"

Shelly shifted, looked up at him with shining eyes. "Maybe I'm not all that anxious for a few hours of sex with a man who sees me as a body, not a person. Or to spend my life with some man I can't imagine except as a potential father and provider. Seems as though everybody I've dated for the past few years has fallen into one or the other of those categories."

"And how do you see me, Shel?"

"Like you said. As a friend. Somebody I can count on, whether I'm happy or sad. Forgive me. I—"

"Hush. You don't need forgiving." He wanted to be there for her, but…

No. He couldn't father her child and walk away, no matter how clinical the process. No way could he live with himself if he deserted his flesh and blood.

He brushed a tear off her cheek. "You'll have your babies. When you do, you'll thank me for telling you no."

"Maybe I'll thank you someday, my friend. But not today." Her smile was bittersweet. "You know, I wouldn't have expected you to sleep with me."

"Hey. That's rotten. You'd have denied me all the fun?"

His cock twitched, as if it had suddenly realized he was in close proximity to a desirable woman who just happened to be his closest friend.

"Fun?"

"Yeah, fun. I haven't done it lately, but if I recall correctly, having sex is fun. I can't imagine anything less arousing than ogling centerfolds while trying to jerk off in some obstetrician's office."

Shelly giggled.

"What? You think that's funny?"

"Yeah. I thought guys liked ogling naked women with big boobs."

It relieved Kurt to see the twinkle coming back into Shelly's eyes. "The operative word, honey, is *women*. Not pictures. Looking at centerfolds quit turning me on when I was about seventeen."

He stood, pulled her up beside him. "Come on now. Let's walk off some of the calories we consumed in those fajitas before I take you home."

* * * * *

Why did he feel as though they'd left questions unresolved when he got called to the hospital less than an hour after Shelly had asked him to father her baby?

After all, Kurt thought as he stripped off bloodstained scrubs and shrugged his tired shoulders, he'd told her no. And she seemed to have accepted his refusal.

Too bad the teenage boy he'd just helped piece back together had chosen tonight to play chicken with an eighteen-wheeler on the outbound expressway. Otherwise he'd have stayed with Shelly, made sure she was really okay.

Kurt's partner, Mark Blackstone, looked exhausted when he came out of the surgeons' shower room, obviously favoring his gimpy leg. Tedious microsurgery like what Mark had performed on their patient's nearly severed arm and hand took as much of a physical toll as muscling displaced fractures back into position and fitting internal fixation devices into shattered bone, which pretty well described what Kurt had done to the kid's mangled legs.

"Hell of a night," Mark observed as he dragged clothes out of his locker.

"I should have known it would be as soon as I noticed a full moon up in the sky. Must be something to that superstition that it brings out crazies as well as babies."

"Yeah. Seems that way, especially on nights like tonight. By the way, how was Shelly's birthday celebration?"

"Other than cut short by the call? Fine. We went to that restaurant across from the Mercado that has strolling guitarists. La Margarita."

"I've got to take Lynn down there soon. She loves to listen to the Spanish music. Thinks it's romantic. On the downside, she also loves spending money in those touristy little shops."

Mark stood. "Speaking of romance, I promised Lynn I'd get home as fast as I could." He pulled a shirt from his locker and shrugged into it.

Kurt took his time in the shower, letting the needles of hot water soothe away the aches he'd acquired while hunched over Bobby Duran's mangled body for almost four hours.

Unlike Mark, he had no reason to hurry home. No reason to care whether he fell onto a cot in the surgeons' lounge or the empty, mussed-up bed at his apartment.

Sometimes he envied his partner, especially late at night when fatigue numbed painful memories of his disastrous marriage. Times like this, regret seeped in for having missed out on so much of Jason's childhood.

His thoughts drifted back to Shelly. She had to be crazy to think she wanted to bring a kid up all by herself.

But then she was a woman. And most women loved babies.

Hell, he loved kids, too. Missed having his son with him all the time.

Kurt and Jason had both lost something irreplaceable when Adrianna had tossed him out. Yeah, he'd been a lousy husband. He'd never denied her accusation that he put his patients first.

He hadn't been able to envision practicing medicine any other way. Lives depended on him putting patients' needs above catering to a spoiled woman's whims.

But he had made time for his son. He still did when he was given the opportunity, no matter what Adrianna claimed.

Banishing his fractured family from his mind, Kurt pulled on clean scrubs. He'd check on Bobby Duran, then grab a few hours' sleep before morning rounds.

And he'd call Shelly and make certain she knew he cared about her. He'd also do his damnedest to talk her out of her crazy scheme.

The idea of her finding somebody else to give her a baby didn't set well. Not well at all.

* * * * *

"Morning, Lynn. Where's Shelly?" Kurt asked a few days later when he stopped by the therapy room to check on a patient's progress.

Lynn smiled. "She took the morning off to settle her sister in at home. I like the charm you gave her for her birthday."

Mark's wife was drop-dead gorgeous, with wavy dark hair and big, chocolate-brown eyes. Unfortunately she had an annoying habit of matchmaking between every eligible man and woman she came across.

Not about to encourage her, Kurt ignored Lynn's comment about his gift.

"I dropped by to check on Mrs. Anderson."

"Not to see Shelly?" Lynn's eyes sparkled, the way Kurt noticed they always did when she thought she smelled a wedding.

"Don't even think about trying to find me a soulmate." Kurt made a show of ogling Lynn, head to toe. "Mark already got the only woman I could ever fall for."

"Right. Well, Dr. Silverman, while you pine away for me, you might want to know Shelly got Mrs. Anderson to take a few steps without her walker yesterday morning."

"Good. I'll drop by again later when Shelly's here." Kurt made a mental note to congratulate his elderly patient for the progress she was making following hip surgery.

"By the way, Mark had me go over to the hospital and assess Bobby Duran for rehab. He said to ask you whether you want us to start passive exercises on his legs."

"Not until the infection's under control."

"Oh. Post-op infection?"

"More like pre-op. Half the asphalt from the beltline expressway was embedded in Mr. Duran. We got the tar out, but apparently some nasty bacteria's still there."

"Ouch."

"Yeah. Ouch." Kurt flipped through the rehab patients' charts and made a few changes to his orders. "If I haven't told you lately, you physical therapists make our jobs a whole lot easier."

When Lynn smiled, a dimple showed in her cheek. "Thanks. Shall I give Shelly your best?"

"Sure."

As Kurt strode toward his office, he felt cheated because he'd missed seeing his pal.

* * * * *

"You missed Kurt while you were out. He stopped by to see you about an hour ago," Lynn said, her tone conspiratorial.

She had to be the world's most incurable romantic.

Shelly shook her head. "Get real. If Kurt stuck his head through that door, it was because he wanted to check on his patients."

"Yes, but he wanted to check on them with you."

"We're friends. And he likes the way I rub his back."

"Mark likes the way I rub his back. Not to mention other more interesting parts of him. Who's to say friends can't also be lovers?"

"So you want me to jump the bones of every patient who likes my back rubs?"

"Certainly not. But Kurt is hardly your patient. Come on, Shelly. Admit you're hot for the man. Admit you'd like him to rub those big talented hands all over you while you taste and stroke and tease him to a sexual frenzy. Tell me you don't ache when he's not around."

"I—I…"

"Kurt doesn't make you want to fuck him half to death?"

"I…don't know. I've never—"

Lynn's mouth dropped open. "You've never what?"

"I've never made love. Hardly ever even been kissed."

Her innocence was certainly not of her own volition. Raised by strict parents in the shadow of her outgoing older sister Donna, Shelly had managed to attract only one boyfriend through high school and college—and he'd married her best friend days before their college graduation. Her record in the ten years since then hadn't been much better.

"Then you really don't know."

No, she didn't. But she wanted to. "Tell me, how does it feel to be turned on?"

"Fantastic. There's some sort of special chemistry that draws you to a particular man. I'll never forget the way I felt the first time Mark kissed me. It was instant fireworks."

Lynn sighed, and she had a dreamy look in her dark eyes. Her cheeks were flushed. "It's still like that. Six years we've been married, and I still go crazy every time he touches me. Hell, sometimes he can get me hot with just a glance. "

Shelly shook her head. Mark Blackstone admittedly was good to look at, and he was nice to boot, but he'd never made *her* see stars. Maybe she just wasn't a "hot" kind of woman.

On the other hand, she'd felt twinges—twinges that got stronger when Kurt was around. Whenever her body accidentally came in contact with his.

Shelly envied Lynn.

* * * * *

Kurt stood in Mark's office that afternoon, waiting to go over Bobby Duran's records before a meeting with Bobby's parents.

He stared at the large, framed photo that had first caught his eye when he came from Atlanta to interview for the group practice opening. Black and white, the candid shot of Mark and Lynn stood out in stark contrast with the blown-up color snapshots of the couple's daughters.

Looking at the photos reminded Kurt of the walls in his own office, bare except for two framed paintings of arid landscapes in southwest Texas.

"Ready to go over treatment plans?" Mark asked as he strode in and settled behind his desk.

"How do you do it?"

"Do what?"

"Manage a career and have enough of yourself left over for Lynn and the kids?"

Mark ran his fingers through his hair. "It's the other way around. Lynn and the girls are my life. I fit in my work around them."

"Sure you do. You put in as many hours here and in surgery as I do."

"Lynn's a surgeon's daughter. She's used to sharing me with the patients." Mark picked up a small, framed photo of his wife in her wedding gown and smiled down at her image. "Before I met her, I'd never imagined a woman could love me the way she does. Or that I'd ever put anything or anyone ahead of my patients."

"You're a lucky SOB."

"Yeah. I am." Mark's expression turned serious when he set the photo down. "What do we tell Duran's parents about his prognosis?"

"That Bobby is damn lucky to be alive. That with a lot more luck he'll be able to use the hand you put back together, at least for tasks that don't require fine motor coordination."

"What about his legs?"

"Let's not give his parents a lot of hope there."

Mark shook his head. "It's awful, a young kid getting torn up the way he was."

"He did it to himself. Did you get a look at his blood alcohol level?"

"No. What was it?"

"Point two-nine. It was a wonder he could find his cycle, much less ride it. How did he look when you saw him this afternoon?"

"Not good. I'd hoped the new antibiotics would have cleared most of the infection up by now."

"Me, too. But I'm not surprised. If we can't get the infection under control soon, Duran will end up with a mid-thigh amputation. Did the latest cultures come back?"

Mark dug through the papers in Bobby's file and found the lab report. "*E. coli.* And some unidentified strain of bacteria that apparently isn't responding to treatment."

Kurt got up, paced, then faced Mark again. "Bobby may not be able to walk, even if we manage to avoid amputation."

"I hate to tell his parents that." Mark ran his fingers through his hair. "I have a pretty good idea what may be going through their heads."

"Memories?"

"Yeah. I think Mom suffered more than I did when I got hurt. It took years before she realized I wasn't going to let a gimpy leg slow me down. You know, I was about Bobby's age when I totaled that Mustang convertible."

Kurt doubted he could gracefully accept an injury as severe as what Mark had suffered in the accident that had resulted in his leg setting off metal detectors in airport security screeners.

"Maybe you should be the one to talk with Bobby's parents," he said. "You know more than I do about how to tell the truth without slaughtering their hopes."

A sharp crackling sound drew his attention to the intercom.

"Doctor Silverman?" The soft feminine voice provided a pleasant contrast with the grating noise that preceded it.

"Yes, Doris?" Kurt got an uneasy feeling. The office manager rarely paged anybody.

"Calvin Crane is here to see you. He says it's urgent."

Kurt glanced at Mark, answered his unspoken question. "My attorney. Without a doubt, the person I least wanted to see today."

"Go see what he wants. I'll handle Bobby's parents. And by the way, I've got five bucks that says the kid will not only keep that leg but also be able to use it."

"Put Crane in my office. I'll be right with him," Kurt told Doris. Then he looked up at Mark. "You're on. But that's one bet I hope I lose."

What the hell was going on?

* * * * *

Kurt knew all too soon. The judge in Atlanta hadn't merely limited his visitation. She'd restricted it even more drastically than Adrianna had requested.

"So what can I do, other than let this judge keep me from seeing my son?"

"Get married."

"'Jump from the frying pan into the fire,' to quote an old cliché?"

Cal shrugged. "Adrianna convinced the judge of all three things she'd alleged in her petition."

"And those things are?" Kurt sat on the couch in a corner of his office and gestured for Cal to join him.

"One, you don't set aside enough time to spend with Jason when he visits. Two, you don't have stable care arrangements for him. Three, your apartment's not fit for your son to visit."

Kurt clenched his fists but refrained from denying the allegations. The all-powerful judge apparently had made up her mind.

"Assuming these things are true, how would my getting married change the situation?"

"Well, I'd argue—and I'm fairly certain the judge would agree—your wife would step in and take over Jason's care and entertainment when your work makes it impossible for you to be with him. Not to mention that a wife would probably insist you buy a house instead of living in that dismal furnished apartment that you call home."

Kurt regretted slamming his fist onto the arm of the sofa when his knuckles sent a sharp protest to his brain. "A housekeeper could do that, too."

"Not according to the judge. Jason apparently told Adrianna that the last woman you hired routinely left him by himself until you got home—sometimes after midnight."

"For God's sake, Cal, I'm a trauma surgeon. I can't schedule accidents to happen during office hours. Besides, Jason's twelve years old. It doesn't hurt him to be by himself in the apartment for an hour or two, once in a while."

"I tried that argument, but it didn't fly." Cal shook his head, then met Kurt's gaze.

"Since I'm certain you aren't going to restrict your surgical practice, I suggest you get yourself a wife. Or resign yourself to seeing your son for a week, twice a year. I've got to get to my office now, but I thought you deserved to hear the bad news in person."

After the lawyer left, Kurt sat and stared at the bare walls of his office.

Get married again? Cal had to be certifiably insane.

Chapter Three

Or was he?

Late that night, as he lay in bed and listened to ambulances come and go from the emergency room two blocks away, Kurt thought about what his attorney had said.

He wasn't cut out for marriage.

He'd proved that time and again during the ten years he'd tried to juggle his high-pressure career with a high-maintenance wife. He'd been a lousy live-in dad, too, or so Adrianna still told him at every opportunity through her man-eating shark of a lawyer.

Still he was better for Jason than no dad at all. At least he thought so.

Lynn and the kids are my life. I fit in my work around them.

Mark's comment rang in Kurt's ears. Maybe, if he hadn't been quite as driven…if Adrianna had at least tried to understand the demands of his job.

Damn. Maybes didn't cut it.

He pounded his pillow with his fists, then shoved it back under his aching head.

Shelly's talented fingers could coax away his aches and pains, if only she were here.

Kurt sighed at the thought. Her hands would soothe and warm him. She'd chase away the demons that wouldn't let him rest.

He pictured her reddish-brown curls, the freckles that dusted her nose and cheeks. Her clean-scrubbed face, more wholesome than beautiful. Deep green eyes that usually sparkled with laughter.

Eyes that had filled with tears when he'd made fun of her request for a favor. A request he'd soon enough realized she was dead serious about.

His cock throbbed. Hell, it had been too long since he'd gotten laid. Here he was, getting a raging hard-on, thinking about his good buddy Shelly.

Funny thing. Thinking about Shelly had never gotten him horny before, but visualizing her now had him hard as a rock and ready to burst.

Maybe it was knowing she wanted him to give her a baby.

Kurt twisted onto his stomach and tried to ignore his cock's urgent demand for satisfaction. That made his balls ache worse.

Damn it, he had one child already that his ex-wife barely allowed him to see. No way would he father one who would only be his in the strictest biological terms.

But what if it weren't? What if he and Shelly could build on their friendship?

What if they were to become a couple? A family?

What if Shelly, unlike Adrianna, could live with the demands of his profession, enjoy the time he had for her and not constantly demand more?

After all, Shelly didn't love him the way Adrianna had sworn she did. He wasn't in love with her, either.

They were friends. Friends supported each other instead of sniping and complaining.

Shelly wanted a baby, and he desperately needed not to lose meaningful contact with his son.

Kurt bolted from the bed.

The clock on the floor said ten past midnight, and he had a three-hour case scheduled to start at eight in the morning.

No matter. He'd never required a lot of sleep.

He had to talk to Shelly, and it wouldn't wait.

* * * * *

Nearly one o'clock. Shelly set down the historical romance she'd been reading and padded to the kitchen, forcing herself not to rub at her gritty eyes.

Maybe a glass of milk would help her sleep.

A loud buzz made her jump. Who could be visiting at this time of night? A bit alarmed, she went to the door and peered through the fisheye.

Kurt?

She looked again. It *was* Kurt. What on earth was he doing here?

She stared down at the oversize T-shirt she had on and finger-combed her hair. Then she unlocked the door and let him in.

"Hi."

In snug, worn jeans that emphasized the impressive bulge between his legs, he looked good. Better than good. Hot, she supposed Lynn would say. But he also looked bone tired. The lines around his mouth and at the corners of his eyes hinted at stress as well as fatigue.

"Shelly. Did I wake you?"

She shook her head. "I was going to the kitchen for a snack. Can I fix you something?"

"No thanks. But you go ahead. Get something for yourself."

A minute later she joined him in the living room, a plate of cookies in hand.

"Here, in case you change your mind." She set the cookies down and curled up at one end of the sofa where she could feast her eyes on broad shoulders and muscular arms that stretched the sleeves of his dark blue polo shirt.

"Did you have an emergency case?"

He shook his head. "Couldn't sleep."

"Want a back rub?" Her fingers itched to touch him, even if it was only to alleviate his discomfort.

"Yeah. I was thinking about your magic fingers. Would you?"

"Sure. Come on, you can lie across my bed. If you'll take off some clothes, I'll use a new brand of deep-heating lotion a sales rep gave me to try out."

He stood beside her bed, toed off his deck shoes and peeled his shirt over his head.

The good-sized room shrank in his presence. It felt downright tiny when he unbuttoned his jeans and skinned them off.

Shelly suppressed a groan.

Kurt looked good enough to eat with all his clothes in place. Naked except for dark socks and white cotton boxer shorts, he took her breath away.

When he found time to work out, she couldn't imagine, but it was obvious from his well-toned muscles that he did.

"How do you want me?"

"What?" Any way she could get him came to mind.

He laughed. "On my stomach or my back?"

"Your stomach. It's your back I'm going to rub down, or did you forget?"

"I didn't forget." He flopped onto the bed, face down, and let out a sigh. "I'm all yours."

She wished.

The lotion she spread onto his back warmed her hands and filled the air with a not-unpleasant hint of menthol. Touching him like this—skin to taut, golden skin—heightened her awareness of each corded muscle, every silky inch of his body. With each motion of her fingers, she felt the tension drain from him.

"Don't stop."

His voice sounded almost like a growl, muffled as it was in the folds of her down comforter. How would he sound if he were in the throes of passion?

What would it be like if he thought of her as more than a friend?

Would he turn over and draw her into his arms? Would his kiss awaken the kind of electrical chain reaction Lynn said happened every time Mark touched her?

As if she'd willed it, he rolled over and met her gaze with stormy eyes.

Embarrassed that he might have guessed her thoughts, Shelly looked away, but Kurt caught her chin, held her captive.

"Kiss me," he said almost as if he was issuing a challenge.

Maybe he was.

There was no way Shelly could resist bending and brushing his lips with her own. When she did, she understood all about hot—all about the sensations the right man can generate inside a woman.

Heightened sensation. The smells and tastes of coffee and his aftershave, the velvety texture of his lips. His breathing and hers, mingled sounds of man and woman and arousal. His tongue, setting her on fire as he traced her lips until he coaxed them open.

He made her want more. Much more.

For a moment she thought their kiss affected him that way, too, until he broke the contact and pulled away.

"You know, Shelly," he said as she began to knead the knotted muscles in his upper arms, "I've been thinking."

"About the way I made an idiot of myself the other night?"

He shook his head. "No. Well, yes and no. I've been thinking about us doing each other a mutual favor."

Her breath caught in her throat when he grabbed and held her hands. "What do you mean?"

"You want a baby. I need help to create and maintain the stable sort of home environment not even Adrianna can claim is bad for Jason." He paused, then continued.

"Marry me and make us a home no one can say is unfit for my son to visit, and I'll do my best to give you that baby you want so much."

"You mean—you want me to live with you? To bring up a family together?"

"Would that be so bad? You probably see more of me every day at the office and the hospital now than you would at home."

"And that would be good?" The gentle motion of his thumb rotating against her palm soothed her jangled nerves.

He scowled. "Maybe not, but I won't put anything or anyone ahead of my patients."

"I wouldn't expect you to." And she wouldn't, no matter how much she might wish she were his number-one priority.

"There's one more thing I'll tell you from the outset. I love you as a friend, but I'm not in love with you and I don't expect you to fall in love with me."

That burst of honesty hurt. A lot.

"I don't know," she said.

"Are you in love with somebody?"

"N-no."

"Then there's no reason we shouldn't get married."

"I guess not." But something vital was missing from Kurt's tidy equation.

He pushed back a lock of hair that threatened to block her vision. "Don't be sad, Shel. Stars-in-your-eyes, head-over-heels love is highly overrated. The stars lose their glow pretty quickly in the light of day. I'd rather have friendship. You won't need to worry that I'll chase women. I honor the vows I make."

"But—"

"I can practically hear your brain grinding away. Yeah, I screwed up one marriage, but you're not Adrianna. You understand what I do, how important it is, how my work can't be confined to a schedule. She didn't. The only time Adrianna ever set foot inside a hospital was to have

Jason. We can make it together because neither of us has any illusions."

He wiped away a tear from her cheek. "We're not kids anymore. I need a wife so the judge will reinstate the visitation schedule she just cut back to damn near nothing. And you need a husband if you want a family."

Yes, she did.

But marriage to a friend who wasn't about to fall in love again? Who didn't want her to love him the way she had a sneaky feeling she already did?

"There are lots of single moms," Shelly pointed out, less confidence in her voice than she'd intended.

"But you don't really want to do it by yourself, do you?"

"Of course not."

She didn't, but his proposition seemed so cold — not at all the declaration of love she'd dreamed of hearing one day along with a heartfelt proposal.

"Kurt, do you want me?"

"Damn it, I just asked you to marry me. Of course I want you."

"I mean, do you want to sleep with me?" Her cheeks burned, and she imagined they had turned beet-red.

His grin warmed her to her toes. "I hadn't thought about it until earlier tonight, but yeah. I want to. We're good friends. We'll be good lovers, too. If we're going to get married and have a baby, there's no reason for us to deny ourselves the fun of having sex."

"Okay." She took his feather-light touch on the upper curve of her breast as a promise, though she had the feeling she was deceiving herself.

"Okay, we'll sleep together, or okay, you'll marry me?"

"I'll marry you." Her stomach knotted up, but she managed a smile. "And I'll sleep with you, too."

"Good. We'll need to make arrangements right away. What time do you get off work tomorrow?"

"Four."

"Barring emergencies, I should be finished with patients by then. We can order pizza at my place and start making plans."

She'd heard operating room nurses at the hospital say Kurt was like a bulldozer, but she hadn't witnessed this side of him until now. Dazed, she watched him slide off her bed and dress with cool efficiency while her head was spinning.

"See you tomorrow, Shel. Thanks for the rubdown."

He shot a grin her way, then bent and kissed her.

Before she could say a word, he was gone.

Her breast still tingled from his casual touch, and the faint, citrusy smell of his cologne swirled around her head.

Married.

Soon he'd touch her everywhere. He'd kiss her and pet her and fill her with his heat and hardness…

Shelly slid her hand under her nightshirt, stroked first one nipple and then the other until they both got hard and pebbly. Hot sensations shot through her, setting off a flood of sensation—and emotions that had her panties damp and her pussy swelling.

Using her other hand, she stroked that hot, wet flesh Kurt would soon discover. Slick. She spread the moisture with one finger, circling her swollen clitoris and sending delicious twinges all the way to her toes.

Soon she'd stroke his muscular shoulders, feel his heavy thighs pushing hers apart. His dark chest hair would tickle her breasts, and he'd bend and kiss her the way he had tonight.

No. He'd take her mouth, consume it, take her breath away. And she'd open to him, and finally she'd know…

All those delicious sensations she'd read about, waited for. Experienced time and again in her dreams.

The tingling. The heat. Like the sensations she was feeling now, first between her legs, spreading cell by cell down her inner thighs, up to curl in her belly and beyond. A quiet little climax, unintended and brought on by her own touch…and fantasizing about the real sex she'd soon share with Kurt.

Had she dreamed his nocturnal visit, or had it been real?

Shelly didn't know for sure until the following afternoon, when Kurt met her outside the door of the physical therapy room and said they had some plans to make.

* * * * *

The pizza was spicy and steaming hot, the beer ice-cold. Kurt polished off a third slice before pulling out a credit card and the wrinkled prescription form where he'd scribbled a list of things that needed doing as they'd come to mind throughout the day.

The damned list included everything from getting blood tests to buying a house. It needed prioritizing as well as whittling down to manageable size.

Which chores could he delegate to Shelly?

His gaze settled on the third entry. Rings. He could give Shel the credit card and tell her to pick out ones she liked.

No he couldn't. Shelly might be his best friend, but that didn't mean she'd appreciate being asked to buy her own engagement ring. He'd do that himself, as soon as he had time.

"Why are you holding onto that VISA card?" Shelly asked, breaking his concentration.

He set down the list and handed her the card. "It's for you. We'll need to buy some things, and you have a lot more free time than I do."

"Okay." She reached for the list, but he held it just outside her range of motion.

"Let's go through this item by item. You can make notes." He handed her a pad and pencil.

She nibbled on the eraser. "Okay, shoot."

"You need to give notice that you'll be leaving work in two weeks," Kurt said, and he crossed off an item from his list.

"You want me to quit my job?"

From the sound of her voice and the look on her face, he got the idea she thought he'd lost his mind. He thought so, too. Her quitting her job would hurt his patients, because she did wonders rehabilitating them following surgery.

He reminded himself that Cal had said a stay-at-home wife would play best with the hard-nosed judge. "I don't want you to, but I think you should." Much as he hated the thought of replacing Shelly at work, he needed every advantage he could get if he was going to get that judge to change her mind.

"And what do you expect me to do until your son or our baby arrives, all week long while you're at work?"

Kurt attempted a grin, though his facial muscles tightened as though they wanted to frown. "You can find us a house. Redecorate it. Join the medical auxiliary at the hospital. Play tennis at the country club. Shop. Redecorate the house again. Shop some more. You'll find plenty to keep you busy. Adrianna did."

Shelly's expression turned stubborn. "I want to keep working. At least part-time. I can't see myself spending my days the way you say your ex-wife did. You should understand how much satisfaction it gives me to help patients regain mobility."

He understood. Truth was, Shelly's dedication to her patients was one of the traits he most admired in her. Maybe…

"You're right. You aren't Adrianna. Thankfully. Maybe you could work half-days. I'll ask Cal."

She frowned. "Who's Cal?"

"Calvin Crane. My attorney."

"What does your lawyer have to do with when or if I work?"

"He says a stay-at-home wife will play better when we ask for more time with Jason. I don't want that judge to have any excuse for keeping my son from spending his summers with us."

"All right. But I can't imagine a judge refusing to let a twelve-year-old live with you because his stepmother has a job."

"Don't worry about it. I'll talk to Cal. After all, you work for my practice, so you can have time off whenever you want. Meanwhile, we need to buy a house. You can start looking for one right away."

"Wait a minute. I have no idea what kind of place you'd like. Or how much you want to spend on it."

Kurt could care less, so long as Shelly didn't pick out some ostentatious pillared monstrosity like the last place he'd lived in Atlanta with Adrianna. He imagined Shelly's taste ran more toward casual than fancy.

"I'll leave the style up to you. After all, you'll be spending more time there than I will. We'll need four or five bedrooms and a pool. Whatever other amenities you think a house should have."

"Is that all?"

He ignored her sarcasm.

"Not quite. The house needs to be in a respectable neighborhood so Adrianna won't have room for complaint, but not too far from the office or the hospital. I don't like the idea of commuting for hours every day."

She lifted her pencil, looked him in the eye. "Do you have a price range in mind?"

"I don't have a clue about what houses cost in San Antonio. I'll pay whatever it takes to get what you want. Within reason, of course."

When she nibbled at her lower lip, he suddenly wanted to nibble on it for her.

"I'll check out some houses, pick some I like, and then we'll look at them together. I'm not about to make a six-figure decision with your money, without your participation. Okay?"

Making unilateral spending decisions had never bothered Adrianna, so Kurt found Shelly's reticence refreshing. "Fine. You'll have to decide about the furniture on your own, though. I don't have time. And I hate traipsing through stores. I don't give a damn what you pick out as long as it suits you and isn't too uncomfortable."

Shelly glanced over her list. "Anything else you want me to take care of?"

"No. I can do the rest." The least he could do was take care of the rings, the license and the wedding itself. Unless…

"You don't have your heart set on a big blowout of a wedding, do you?"

"No. Except for Donna, I'm on my own. My parents died several years ago. What about your family?"

"They won't come. Dad's been in a wheelchair for twenty years, and Mom's not well either. My sister and her husband live with them."

"Is your dad's condition the reason you went into trauma surgery?"

"Partially. He could have gotten better care than he did. Anyhow, I thought so at the time, but then I was just a kid. I don't see much of my family."

Uncomfortable discussing family from whom he had been more or less estranged since marrying Adrianna, Kurt reached over and took Shelly's hand. "It will be just us, your sister and brother-in-law, and a couple of witnesses. Will that be okay?"

She smiled and nodded, but Kurt wondered if she wished deep down for some pomp and ceremony. He couldn't help recalling the three-ring circus Adrianna had insisted on even though she'd been noticeably pregnant at the time.

"How about us asking Lynn and Dr. Blackstone to be our witnesses?" she asked, apparently okay with the idea of the no-frills ceremony.

"Fine." Maybe the happiest couple he'd ever seen together would rub off a little of their magic on him and Shelly. "Is next week too soon?"

She met his gaze. "It is quick. What do you think?"

"Sooner the better." If he didn't just do it, he'd lose his nerve.

Damn, Kurt didn't want to lose Shelly's friendship, but he suspected that might happen when she discovered how deficient he was in the qualities that made a decent husband and dad.

Shelly jotted the date they selected onto her pad. "Donna and her husband should be able to come, too. She's getting around pretty well already."

Kurt's conscience prodded him. Shelly deserved more of a wedding than a few words in a judge's office with only the state-required pair of witnesses and a couple of other guests.

Maybe she'd enjoy a honeymoon of sorts.

"I can arrange for us to take a few days off, if you'd like to take a trip."

When she smiled, her eyes sparkled. "I'd like that."

"Then we'll do it. Mark will cover for me. I've done double duty for him enough times." Kurt leaned over and brushed his lips across the corner of her mouth. "It's your call. Beach or mountains?"

Her expression pensive, she took another sip of beer and licked the foam off her upper lip. He'd seen her do that a hundred times but suddenly the gesture seemed incredibly erotic. Kurt's balls tightened, and blood rushed to his cock.

Suddenly the idea of having Shelly all to himself, with no cell phones or beepers to intrude, seemed not only prudent but imperative. They'd fuck slow and easy, hard and fast. He'd make her scream with pleasure in a hundred ways.

If he could still remember how it was done.

"Let's go to the mountains."

He imagined Shelly meant the Rockies. But he had a better idea. "I think I know where we can go. One of the anesthesiologists I used to work with in Atlanta has a cabin in the Great Smoky Mountains. Spring's just around the corner there. It's too warm for winter sports and there's probably not a lot to do…"

"It sounds wonderful. You work so hard, you need rest, not a jumble of tourist-y stuff."

"Rest? I was thinking I need to get to know you in the biblical sense. See how many times I can make you come while I'm doing my best to follow through with my part of our bargain."

"Oh."

The flush on Shelly's cheeks made her look so innocent, Kurt wondered for a minute if she might still be a virgin. Then he discarded that idea.

It was ridiculous. Shelly was an attractive woman, and she was thirty-two years old. He doubted she'd had a lot of sexual experience, but a virgin? No way.

After she went home, insisting he not follow in his car when he so obviously needed sleep, Kurt wandered around his apartment. The emptiness of the rooms unnerved him, made him consider how Shelly had made her small apartment seem like home.

He considered going over there and sharing the double bed that would hardly accommodate his six-foot-plus height. Getting a head start on the project of making her a mom.

His balls ached, and his cock hardened. His nostrils flared as he breathed in a hint of her flowery perfume that lingered in the air.

His skin prickled when he thought about her talented hands rubbing and kneading away the tension that plagued him at the end of the day. Tension that now centered between his legs.

Kurt swore quietly as he stripped down and stepped into the shower. He'd spent two years without feeling the slightest urge to fuck Shelly Ware. Surely he could control his libido for two weeks, now that it had suddenly sprung to life.

Wrapping his fist around his aching cock, he stood under the warm spray and jerked off. Though he tried to put Shelly out of his mind and focus on nothing but achieving physical release, her image kept taunting him.

He imagined her going down on him, sucking his cock deep down her throat while he sank his fingers into her soft ginger-colored curls.

Would her pussy hair be as bright as the hair on her head? Would it feel crisp or soft beneath his fingers? Briefly he imagined her pussy shaved the way Adrianna had kept hers.

No. She'd just be neatly trimmed. And responsive. His cock swelled in his hand at the thought of her lying under him, her long slender legs wrapped tight around his hips. Riding him while he played with her small tits. The nipples would tighten the way he'd seen them do beneath her swimsuits—and he'd suck first one and then the other.

He had to come. Now. Had to quit torturing himself. Quit fantasizing about fucking Shelly.

Quickly, efficiently, he took care of his immediate problem, savoring the feeling of relief when his balls tightened, then relaxed when he came. But when he stared at the sparkling water cascading over his softening cock, he imagined how much better it would feel buried inside his good friend's welcoming pussy.

Later, as he lay in the dark, he vowed not to mistake lust for love. He'd give Shelly his name, his child, his money—everything but the power to rip out his soul.

Chapter Four

Kurt had been aroused when he kissed her goodnight. And he'd teased her about wanting to spend their honeymoon in bed.

Apparently he was serious about looking forward to them having sex. He obviously thought he needed her to help ensure him reasonable visitation with his son.

But Shelly had few illusions. Kurt didn't love her the way she wanted to be loved.

She was settling.

She knew it, and it hurt—but not so much that she'd refuse Kurt's businesslike offer of marriage and motherhood.

Sleep was the last thing on her mind. Her book lay on the table along with the newspaper she'd picked up in the lobby a few minutes earlier. She picked up the paper and glanced through the real estate section.

Kurt's order was for a good neighborhood close to the hospital. None existed in the immediate vicinity, but she assumed the area around San Antonio's two private colleges wouldn't be too far away for him to drive.

"Ouch." The advertised price of a five-bedroom ranch style house located a few blocks north of the interstate bypass near Trinity University took her breath away.

Maybe they'd need her salary to swing buying a house. Shelly hoped so.

Just because Adrianna had been a stay-at-home wife didn't mean she had to be. She tried to picture herself, rattling around alone with nothing to do but look for ways to amuse herself. The picture wouldn't focus.

Of course, if she had a baby to take care of, that would be different. And Kurt had said he'd do his best to provide her with one, starting on the honeymoon she hadn't dared to hope he'd suggest.

She circled a few ads, then set the paper aside when she started getting sleepy. Tomorrow would be soon enough to start the serious house hunting.

Yawning, she got up and went to bed. The faint smell of Kurt's aftershave lingered on the covers from last night, tickling her nose when she burrowed into a goose down pillow. Pretending he was there beside her, touching her, she stroked lightly over her nipples. They beaded up, sending tiny shock waves deep into her belly and making her whole body ache.

Last night she'd given herself a little climax. She could do it again, but then…

With Kurt—wanting him the way she did, the way she had for years—sex shared would make her solitary pleasures pale by comparison.

She couldn't wait—yet satisfying herself again didn't appeal now, when she could let the tension build up for next week. For her wedding night with the man of her dreams. Never mind that his feelings for her were only friendship—and maybe lust.

Curling on her side, Shelly inhaled deeply, let her hand relax against her breast, and went to sleep.

* * * * *

The next morning over coffee and rolls, Shelly told Lynn she and Kurt were getting married. Knowing her friend well, she braced herself for an onslaught of questions.

She wasn't disappointed. It was as though hers and Kurt's was a love match and Lynn had engineered it all. In the process, Lynn added to Shelly's already burgeoning list of things to do.

"If you and Kurt want a house close to the university, you should look at one that just went on the market. It's a couple of streets over from where we live, and it's gorgeous."

"I don't know. The prices out there are awfully steep."

"You said Kurt didn't want a long drive. Well, unless you want to restore some relic near downtown—"

"Kurt also said the house has to be in a good neighborhood, or he may not be able to have Jason come and stay."

"Then he has to have some idea about what this house is going to cost."

Shelly didn't think so. "He sounded as if he didn't care. As a matter of fact, he gave me the impression that so long as the place has a swimming pool and at least four bedrooms, he doesn't much care what it looks like."

"Well, he'll like the place I've got in mind. And I doubt it would pauper him to buy it unless he's stuck paying a fortune in alimony. We'll look it over, and then we'll take a little shopping trip. You're going to need a wedding dress, not to mention some sexy things to take on your honeymoon."

"I'll have to check with Kurt. He might want us to do something."

"Nonsense. He didn't say he wanted to go somewhere with you tonight, did he?"

"No."

"I didn't think so. He, Mark, and some other surgeons have a six o'clock meeting scheduled with the hospital administrator. They're trying to wring money out of him for some new, state-of-the-art lasers and 'scopes for the OR."

"Oh." Maybe after they were married, Kurt would let her in on his schedule.

"You'd better pray they get the new toys they want. Last time Kurt came over, he and Mark spent half the evening complaining that they had to do all sorts of operations with prehistoric tools. They described them in pretty graphic detail. Made for less than appetizing dinner conversation."

Shelly could imagine. "All right. We'll take a look at this house."

"And shop? I'll need to call the kids' nanny and let her know I won't be home until late. Believe me, shopping's not something you want to do with two preschoolers along."

What would Kurt think if she got herself all fancied up for him? Shelly doubted he'd even notice.

Still, this was going to be her only wedding. Her only honeymoon. And Lynn could give her advice on the sort of lingerie Mark liked. She had the feeling Kurt's taste would be similar.

"I'd like to buy a few things—a nightgown or two, some new slacks and tops for the trip, stuff like that. But I don't need a wedding gown. It's not going to be that kind of a wedding."

"Any wedding's that kind if you want it to be," Lynn said, her tone nostalgic as though she might have been recalling her own.

"You're right. I'll see if I can find a new suit. Nothing fancy, though."

Shelly wished Lynn weren't so insistent, but part of her looked forward to house hunting and shopping—and the big changes that were coming in her life.

* * * * *

"I will say, once you make up your mind to do something, you don't waste time." Mark watched the jeweler at the shop across the street from the hospital as he totaled up the bill for the rings Kurt had chosen. "You're going to do it next week?"

Kurt wiggled his little finger, watched the light play off the two-carat diamond solitaire that rode against his first knuckle.

"Yeah. A colleague from Atlanta is lending me his mountain cabin near Knoxville, Tennessee. The wedding will be Wednesday afternoon, and Shel and I will leave right afterward. I'll be back the following Monday."

"Sure you don't want a few more days off? You've covered a lot longer than five days at a time for me."

"Five days is plenty."

Mark laughed. "I don't understand you, my friend. Lynn and I took three weeks for our honeymoon, and if I could have, I'd have added on three more."

"Maybe I work faster than you. Or maybe I intend for the honeymoon to last long after we get home." So far Mark and Lynn seemed to think this was a love match, and Kurt would just as soon keep them thinking that way. Better for him—and for Shelly—than if their co-workers knew they were doing each other a mutual favor.

"Whatever you say. We'd better hurry if we're going to make that meeting on time."

Kurt glanced at his watch, then slid the ring off his finger and set it into its slot in a dark green velvet box beside the matching band. He scribbled his name on the charge slip, pocketed the small box, and hurried to catch up with Mark.

* * * * *

"Get this one. It's so sexy, Kurt will drool."

Shelly doubted that. But the shimmery peach silk gown reflected the lamplight in the lingerie boutique. Soft-looking ivory lace inlays in the empire bodice kept the deceptively simple garment from being fully transparent, and a matching bikini panty veiled the bare essentials down below.

"I like it." She hoped she wouldn't embarrass herself with Kurt by trying so hard to turn him on.

Lynn nodded, the gown apparently forgotten as she turned back to the rack and found a matching robe, a slightly heavier, darker textured silk with sleeves made from the same ivory lace as the inlays on the gown.

"This will be my treat." She grinned. "For Kurt."

"I hope he appreciates what we're doing to jump-start his sex drive." Shelly added half-a-dozen bras and an equal quantity of lacy underwear to a growing pile. "I probably would never have thought to replace my good old cotton undies if you hadn't suggested it."

"Kurt will appreciate the view, though I don't imagine his cock will need any help. Just thinking about getting it on usually does the trick for guys—at least it does for Mark."

After they'd paid for their purchases and gone outside, Shelly turned to Lynn. "Had you and Mark had sex before—"

"On our second date. And every chance we got after that. But then I was no virgin, and Mark needed reassurance that his body turned me on, not off."

"I don't think Kurt has any problem with self-assurance."

Shelly had trouble picturing Mark Blackstone ever having had anything less than a hefty and healthy ego, either. But Lynn hadn't elaborated and Shelly didn't feel right about asking. She assumed the reticence Lynn had mentioned must have had something to do with whatever made him limp when he was tired.

Lynn laughed out loud. "I'm fairly sure Kurt has never entertained the notion that anyone might find him anything except *Número Uno*, physically speaking anyhow. Does he know?"

"You mean does he know I've never had sex before? No. Should I tell him?"

As though that question required some thinking, Lynn paused, her brow furrowed. "Well, he might like finding out for himself. Then again, he might not. I think I'd let him know beforehand."

"He'll think I'm some kind of freak. Thirty-two years old and still untouched."

"More likely, he'll be flattered that you've saved it for him. Here, put your loot back here." She opened the rear door, then moved aside.

Shelly stared at the modest stack of bags and boxes. The clothes she'd maxed out her credit cards to buy hardly made a dent in the spacious rear compartment of Lynn's sport utility vehicle.

Her friend's optimism usually proved infectious. It didn't this time. As Shelly climbed into the passenger seat, her worry threatened to escalate into panic.

"What if this doesn't work out? What if Kurt's son can't stand me?" What if she couldn't keep Kurt interested enough in her to stick with the bargain they'd made?

"Quit worrying. You'll do fine. Jason will take right to you, and before you know it, you'll have father and son both eating out of your hand." With that, Lynn fastened her seat belt and started the engine.

* * * * *

"Lynn said Shelly liked that house they looked at," Mark told Kurt as he hooked his cell phone back onto his belt.

"Good. I guess I can live with the commute."

"The drive isn't bad. Fifteen or twenty minutes, most days. Ten when it's not rush hour."

"Is Shelly still at your place?" Kurt checked his pants pocket, felt the little velvet box. He wanted to give the solitaire to her now, watch her face light up with surprise and, he hoped, pleasure.

"She left about a half-hour ago. Should be home unless she stopped off somewhere." Mark paused in the parking lot, dug in his pocket for his keys. "Want a ride?"

Kurt shook his head. "Thanks anyhow. I'll walk. I need the exercise after sitting for three hours listening to Simpson cry about how broke the hospital is."

Mark slid into the Jaguar sedan that he'd once told Kurt had been his compromise between the sports cars he loved and the family vehicle he had to have for the times he hauled his little girls around. He gunned the engine, then let the window down. "At least we're getting some of the equipment we asked for."

"I'll try to remember that when I have to use that arthroscope Simpson won't replace. It would serve him right if I had to use it on him."

"Yeah, it would. But we'll get the new 'scope next time around. See you in the morning." With that, Mark raised the window and put the Jag in gear.

That was another thing Kurt would have to buy. A car. Two of them, he amended when he remembered the rattletrap Shelly drove. His pride and joy, a classic forty-year-old Alfa Romeo coupe he'd bought while in college and spent years restoring, was too temperamental for daily commuting, not to mention that he didn't want to risk it in expressway traffic.

He'd call the Mercedes dealer tomorrow, see what kind of deal he could make on a pair—a sporty two-seater for himself and a sport utility for Shelly. Or maybe a small sedan. As he let himself into the foyer of her building, he made a mental note to ask her which she'd rather have. And to let her know their house would need a garage for at least three cars.

* * * * *

"Shel?" he called out when she didn't answer the door.

"Just a minute." She sounded breathless.

Kurt imagined her dripping wet from her shower, wrapped up in an oversized towel and trying to hold onto it while running for the door. By the time she opened the door, his cock was primed and ready.

She smiled up at him. "I wasn't expecting you tonight, but come on in."

His guess wasn't far off. She'd obviously been in the shower, but instead of a towel, she had on another giant-sized T-shirt, pale green and clinging to damp, otherwise naked skin. She smelled of coconuts and something else tropical and sweet.

Innocent yet erotic.

His balls tightened, and his cock strained against the zipper of his slacks.

He'd seen Shelly a thousand times, several when she'd had on less than she was wearing now. But those times had been before the idea of making her pregnant had apparently fired up his previously dormant sex drive.

"Don't you want to come in?"

That wasn't anywhere near all he wanted, but he stepped inside. When he started to speak, his voice wouldn't cooperate.

"Kurt, what's wrong?"

Everything. But she'd think he'd gone nuts if he told her he'd suddenly started seeing his good buddy Shelly as a sex object. Big time. "Nothing. I brought you a surprise. Want it?"

She grinned. "Is it Mr. Simpson's head on a platter?"

"Not quite. We did get some of what we asked for, so I thought I'd let him live. I hear you liked the house you looked at with Lynn."

"Sit down. I'll tell you all about it."

"In a minute. First, you sit."

She shrugged, then sank onto the sofa and curled her long legs up under her butt, apparently unaware she'd given him a sneak peek at her pussy.

A pussy just made for his aching cock. He tried to put that pink, inviting flesh with its soft-looking, ginger-colored muff out of his mind, with limited success.

"Okay, now I'm sitting. What's my surprise?" Her eyes sparkled with obvious anticipation.

He hunkered down in front of her where the view was even better and almost forgot what it was he intended to do. Then he took her left hand and slid the ring onto her finger. "This. Like it?"

She did a double take, screamed, and threw her arms around him. The impact sent them tumbling backward onto the floor, her on top of him. His arms closed around her, and their lips locked in a hot, wet kiss.

Already about to burst before they'd touched, he lost control when her soft breasts bored into his chest and her firm silky thighs made an inviting spot to warm his enthusiastic cock.

He'd rolled them over and insinuated a knee between her legs when sanity intervened and made him disentangle their bodies.

"A simple 'yes, thank you' would have sufficed," he ground out, his back turned to her while he adjusted the fit of slacks that hadn't been made to accommodate a raging hard-on.

"Sorry." She sounded injured.

Had she wanted more? Hell, any more and he'd have had his pants off and his cock inside her right there on the hardwood floor.

"Shel, I'm the one who's sorry. I don't know what's come over me in the past few days, but I'm having one hell of a time keeping my hands and other body parts to myself."

"You are?"

"Yeah. And you aren't helping me by running around half-naked."

She looked down at herself, her expression scandalized when she apparently noticed the hard nubs of her nipples poking at the thin material. "I didn't think. But you've seen me in my sleep shirt before. Oh, my God. Why didn't you tell me? You must have thought I wanted —"

"To seduce me? I never thought that at all. Hell, we were good buddies. We still are. It wasn't until we decided to get married that my cock started doing my thinking for me."

Her gaze drifted down to his distended fly, then shot back up as her cheeks turned fiery red. "I'm sorry. I didn't know."

"Well, now you do."

"Does it hurt?"

She sounded so serious that he couldn't help laughing. "I'll live."

"Would you like to —"

"You're damn right I'd like to. But I'm not going to do it. I went into my first marriage with a pregnant bride, and it turned into a disaster. I'm superstitious enough to think bad history might repeat itself. Being horny's not a terminal condition. I can wait three more days."

Her blush spread to her chest and arms when she realized he'd noticed her taking another surreptitious look at the bulge in his pants.

"It may look like I'm going to explode, but I won't. Go put on a robe or something, and then come back and tell me about this house Lynn took you to see."

* * * * *

He liked the sleek, contemporary lines and the casual feel of the place when Shelly dragged him there the following day after they'd applied for a marriage license. There was an extra garage bay for his Alfa, and a library lined with walls of bookshelves where he could hole up and work or read.

Looking out over the neatly manicured and landscaped lawn that surrounded a freeform pool, Kurt considered the aerobic exercise he could get by maintaining the yard himself. He came to his senses, though, and made a mental note to get input from Mark about reliable lawn services in the neighborhood.

Shelly reminded him of a delighted kid, the way she was poking into every nook and cranny in the huge kitchen and family room.

"Want to look around some more before you make up your mind?" he asked.

"Maybe we should. What do you think?"

"You like this place, don't you?"

She grinned. "Who wouldn't? It is awfully expensive, though."

"I can afford it. And I doubt we'll find a place I'd like better. Let's buy this. You can start furnishing it the way you want, as soon as we get back from our trip."

"Are you sure it's not too..." She glanced down at the ring he'd given her. A frown creased her brow as though she thought he'd already shoved himself over the brink toward poverty.

"I'm sure. Just because I've chosen to live in a rat hole since I've been in San Antonio doesn't mean I'm broke. I earn as much or more than most specialty surgeons, and I've been at it nearly ten years. Want to go over my financial statements?"

Her frown disappeared, replaced by a self-deprecating grin. "I probably wouldn't understand them. I've always been pretty much a paycheck-to-paycheck kind of girl. Your accountant deducts my savings and retirement money from my pay before I see it. What's left, I feel free to spend as I see fit."

He was going to like living here with Shelly. From the comments she made as they took another walk-through, Kurt figured she wanted to make the house a cozy home, not a showplace he wouldn't dare step inside without taking off his shoes at the door.

She paused at the door to the small room adjoining the master bedroom. "Nursery or office?"

"Nursery. Unless you want your own private space. If I bring work home, it will mostly involve reading or researching on the Internet. I'll do it downstairs in the library."

"I'm thinking the kitchen will be my office. I can't believe all the room—or that huge walk-in refrigerator. The view of the pool and backyard takes my breath away."

Her enthusiasm was contagious. "Then we'll make this into a nursery. I'll feel more comfortable, knowing we can hear the little guy when he needs something. We can re-do one of the guest rooms for him when he's two or three years old."

"Guy? He?"

"Figure of speech. Boy or girl, makes no difference to me. Let's do the room at the far end of the hall for Jason, though. He's big enough that I don't want him sleeping anywhere near our room."

"Because he likes loud music?"

He brushed a stray curl off her cheek, savoring the feeling of slow arousal that curled through his body. "That, too. Mainly, I don't want us to have to get inhibited. Better that kids be fifty yards or so away once they're old enough to have an idea about what we're doing in bed. And trust me, I'm going to make you scream with pleasure. Often."

"Oh." A fierce blush accompanied her monosyllabic reply. At about the same moment, his cell phone rang.

After dropping Shelly off at Lynn and Mark's place, Kurt drove to the hospital. For the first time in recent memory, he wished he hadn't gotten an urgent call from the ER.

His friend's—no make that his fiancée's—shy reaction to his teasing brought one question foremost on his mind. Could Shelly be half as innocent as she seemed?

And would she take to the enthusiastic sex life his cock and balls were actively anticipating?

He'd find out soon enough.

Chapter Five

The wedding took ten minutes, max.

Shelly wanted to pinch herself. She'd just married the man of her dreams, and he'd gone out of his way to make their simple ceremony memorable.

"You're beautiful," he'd said when he handed her a nosegay.

Though she knew she wasn't, Kurt had sounded so sincere she almost believed he found her so. Maybe the sweet smell of gardenias and orange blossoms in her bouquet had enveloped him in the pleasant haze that had seemed to surround them as they'd said their vows.

Shelly had thought Kurt was handsome in OR scrubs, impressive in casual wear. Sexy as sin in nothing but those white boxers that contrasted with his satiny golden skin.

He was lethal to her senses, though, dressed in a pale gray suit with stark white shirt and a simply patterned blue and gray tie. The pale colors emphasized his dark good looks, while the custom fit of the suit accentuated the hard body she'd seen, touched—and soon would get to feel, up close and personal.

They'd kissed before, but those kisses hadn't prepared Shelly for the sensations that coursed through her veins when Kurt took her in his arms after the judge pronounced them man and wife. The heat he generated with that kiss stayed with her, warmed her while they accepted congratulations from the judge and their four guests. Remembering those hot, tingly feelings helped calm her jittery nerves during the three-hour flight that followed.

* * * * *

Picture-book perfect, Gatlinburg, Tennessee didn't bustle with activity the way she'd imagined it would, but that was all right. It was late for winter sports and early for mountain-climbing devotees to flock to the big chalet and smaller resorts. Shelly had noticed some of the shops were closed when they stopped to pick up a few groceries.

What a gorgeous day! Cool enough to make her skin form goose bumps, the mountain breeze still felt so good Shelly wouldn't close the window as they wound their way up a steep incline. Lush pine and cedar trees lined the two-lane road Their clean, earthy fragrance tickled her nostrils, and the dark green foliage provided a filter for the warm afternoon sun.

"Are you watching for our road?" Kurt asked.

She glanced at the road signs and then at the map Kurt's friend had drawn. "That should be it, up ahead. Hope Mountain Road."

"Okay." The muscles in his forearms contracted when he made a hard right turn onto a narrow, winding road that led up one of the smaller mountain slopes, one without a ski lift swaying in the breeze.

As they got higher, the road turned from asphalt to gravel. Fewer houses peeked through ever-thickening curtains of lush green pines and budding hardwood trees on both sides of them. A deer darted across the road in front of them, and every now and then Shelly spied a patch of snow that hadn't quite given up and melted.

When Kurt's friend had said this cabin was secluded, he'd meant it. The rental Jeep groaned when Kurt downshifted and engaged the four-wheel drive.

"I'd hate trying to get up here when there's snow on the ground, but that's when George comes here the most. How much farther?"

Shelly looked at the map, then scanned the road. "He says to look for a mailbox set into a huge gray boulder."

"That's it up there."

He gave the Jeep more gas, but it didn't speed up. Its rear wheels tossed gravel, creating a crunching sound that echoed off faraway mountains.

"In a hurry?" she asked.

The look he sent her way was pure seduction. "Aren't you?"

She didn't know. Part of her wanted to hold on to the friendship they'd nurtured. The other part—the part that was still simmering from the promise of his kiss in the judge's office—was eager to move on, learn what books couldn't teach about sex and sensuality, what no one had ever described adequately to her in words.

"Shelly?"

"What?" He'd stopped in front of an A-frame cabin braced on stilts against the mountainside.

His smile held a wealth of promise. "I asked if you were anxious to get here, too."

Speechless at the panorama of valleys and mountains before her, she nodded.

Anxious was the operative word. Her pulse raced. She gathered her purse and swung her legs around but couldn't make herself take that next step.

If only she didn't have this awful fear that by becoming Kurt's lover, she'd lose her best friend.

Kurt set their luggage down by the front door of the cabin and fished in his pocket for the key George had given him.

"Okay, Shel. Time for your free ride over the threshold."

But when he turned around to scoop her into his arms, she wasn't there.

He glanced back at the Jeep, saw her sitting there, her sexy legs dangling out the door. She looked damn near scared to death.

Of him? He discarded that notion as absurd, strode over to her and watched her twist around the sparkling band he'd slid onto her finger hours earlier.

"Hey, it's just me. We're buddies, remember."

The slight upturn of her pretty lips left a lot to be desired as reassurance that she was okay, but at least she made the effort to smile.

"I'm afraid."

"The mountain view has your stomach doing flip-flops? Come on, you'll feel better once we get inside."

She gave him her hand, slid off the seat. But she didn't move. She might as well have been glued to the square of graveled drive outside the open door of the jeep.

Though the sun was low in the western sky, her pupils seemed dilated when she looked him in the eye. "It's not the view, Kurt, it's us. What we're doing. I don't want us to ruin our friendship, and I'm terrified that we will."

He'd lost some sleep about that, too, at first. Until he'd promised himself he wouldn't let it happen. Now it seemed he needed to reassure Shelly, so he laid both hands gently on her trembling shoulders.

"We won't. If we weren't best friends, we wouldn't be here. Who but my best friend would I trust enough to marry after the hell Adrianna put me through? And who else but your best pal would you ask to give you a baby?"

Her smile seemed real, but Kurt sensed she wasn't altogether convinced. He glanced at the cabin, then back at her.

"We'll always be friends. We just added another dimension to our friendship with the promises we made today. And we'll go one step further when we get inside and start getting physical."

She squeezed his hand. "You're right. I don't know what's gotten into me."

"Bridal nerves. Come on, let's tackle them head-on." He scooped her up and carried her inside, not stopping until he'd reached the bedroom.

After he set her down, she stared at the king-size bed as if it were an alien being. "Are we going to do it now?"

From her tone Kurt surmised that she'd prefer later. Much later. His cock disagreed, but he'd give her the breathing room it seemed she needed.

"Not yet, Shel. But soon. Let me get our bags and close the door before some critter decides to join us."

When he brought their luggage in a couple of minutes later, she was still standing in the same spot, clutching her purse and nibbling on her lower lip.

"Is it the idea of sleeping with me that has you as jumpy as a patient in the OR that the floor nurse forgot to give his pre-op meds?"

With a show of bravado, Shelly set her purse on the dresser, then met his gaze and shot him a shaky smile. "Hardly. Remember, we slept together before, that night when a storm came up and you didn't want to drive home from Padre Island. The motel just had one vacant room."

"Yeah, we slept in the same bed. But we didn't have sex." Hard to believe he hadn't even thought about that then, considering that his cock was clamoring for her now.

She averted her gaze. "I know."

"Is it sex with me or sex, period, that you're dreading?"

"It's not you. I can't imagine anybody I'd rather...have sex with than you. I'm not afraid, just worried that I won't be able to satisfy you."

"That's not likely to be a problem. Anyhow, let me do the worrying. All you need to do is relax and have fun. You have done this before, haven't you?"

She sat on the edge of the bed, stared down at her feet. "No." For a minute she didn't move, didn't say another word. When she looked up at him, though, she had tears in her eyes. "Go ahead and say it. I'm an oddity. A freak. What else would you call a thirty-two-year-old virgin?"

Shelly might as well have balled up a fist and slammed it into his gut. For a moment he couldn't find his voice. When he did, he spoke carefully.

"Choosy? Discriminating? Maybe cautious?" He sat beside her, stroked the velvety underside of her arm, and tried like hell to ignore his throbbing hard-on.

That was fucking impossible. When she nibbled at her lower lip again, he wanted to taste her there.

"I find you incredibly arousing," he murmured. When the hell had he become a master of understatement?

"Yeah, right. It's arousing to find out I don't know beans about how to please you? Why do I think you're only trying to make me feel better?"

"Because you're about to do something entirely new. I'm nervous, too. I've never had a virgin, and I want it to be good for you." Even if going slow and easy killed him.

He cupped her chin, tilted her face upward, and traced the seam of her lips with his tongue. "You taste good. Sweet."

When her eyelids fluttered and closed, he deepened the kiss. Ignoring his aching balls and throbbing cock, he concentrated on exploring her mouth and testing the softness of her smooth jaw and neck with his fingers.

As if of its own accord, his hand drifted down, cupped her breast. He brushed her tight little nipple with the pad of his thumb. Although a voice inside his head warned him to slow down, take it easy, he tried to ignore it.

But he couldn't. Reluctantly he broke the embrace.

Tears glistened in her eyes. She was breathing hard.

So was he. And his cock felt like it was going to burst if he didn't come soon.

She met his gaze and smiled. Funny, he'd never noticed before that the deep green of her eyes was hot, not cool the way the color green was meant to be.

He caressed lips swollen from his kiss, cheeks reddened and hot where his whiskers had abraded her silky skin.

Damn. He should have shaved first. He'd scratched her with his late-afternoon stubble.

But part of her flush had to be because she was turned on. He'd felt her shy response.

Wondering when he'd turned masochistic, he caught her trembling hand and laid it over his fly. "Feel how you arouse me."

"Oh." She slid her palm along the length of his cock, then tentatively curled her fingers around it. "You're...huge."

And he was getting bigger every second. Ready to burst, more like it, especially when she gave him a tentative squeeze. He had to ease the sexual tension. If he didn't, he'd lose control.

He tweaked a nipple through her clothes, felt it harden, then turned his attention to the other. "Turn about's fair play," he whispered when she let out a little gasp.

She gave him another playful squeeze. "I'll bet I'd like playing with this even more without your jeans in the way. What do I call it?"

Kurt stifled a groan. "You took anatomy, too. Don't tell me you don't know."

"Oh, I know the clinical term, but what do I call it? How do I ask if I can play with your...whatever?"

"It's my cock. Some guys give theirs names, but I never bothered." He watched her cheeks turn bright pink. "Or you can just have at it. My cock is your cock. You don't need to ask."

"Ever?"

"Not when we're alone."

She moved her hand. But not for long. Only long enough for her to unfasten his belt buckle and unbutton his jeans. The zipper hissed when she wrestled it over his distended flesh.

When she shoved his shorts down and took him in her hand, he groaned.

"I always wondered. Now I know."

"Know what?" Her gentle fingers felt hot as fire. It was all he could do not to tumble her backward onto the bed and consummate their vows with all the finesse of a rutting beast.

"That you're magnificent all over. You know, every time I watched you on the beach or rubbed the kinks out of your gorgeous muscles, I used to imagine what you'd look like naked."

Kurt had a healthy ego, and hearing her admit she'd always found him sexually attractive fed it so well that it damn near killed him to hold back. But he was determined to make bells ring for her on her wedding night. And to do that he had to maintain the iron control that made him a top-notch surgeon.

He stilled her hand and brought it to his lips.

"Time out, Shel. Let's take a break. You've got me ready to explode, and I haven't even begun to do the things I want to do with you."

* * * * *

Kurt hadn't needed to shave again. Not really.

Shelly liked feeling the rasp of his five o'clock shadow against her skin.

But he'd insisted. And suggested she heat the barbecued chicken they bought at the market in town.

He might have been hungry, but Shelly's stomach was tied in knots. Anticipation did that to her. So did the lingering fear that she'd disappoint him as a lover, despite his protests to the contrary.

She paced the length of the rustic cabin, then tried to calm her nerves by watching the sun sink behind some mountain peaks that rose in the distance beyond a wooded valley. She had nothing to do but wait for the meat to warm and Kurt to finish shaving. Nothing at all, except anticipate the night ahead.

Kurt would be a thoughtful lover, just as he'd always been her thoughtful friend. Her earlier worries that he might not be able to summon the necessary enthusiasm to have sex with her had proven groundless, but Shelly didn't delude herself into fantasizing that her irresistible charm was what had suddenly turned him on.

More likely his promise to give her a baby fueled his sudden ardor—not to mention his avowed distaste for the process of accomplishing that in any but the time-honored old-fashioned way.

"Penny for your thoughts." Kurt's deep voice pierced the silence. His long fingers rested easily on Shelly's shoulders and sent a spark of awareness coursing through her veins.

She turned, met his expectant gaze. "I was watching the sunset. It seems like we're up in the clouds, miles from civilization. A few minutes ago a flock of geese flew by. It reminded me of airplanes flying in tight formation. You know, like the Air Force pilots did at that show we saw at the Air Force base last fall."

"The Thunderbirds. It would have been something, seeing geese doing rolls and turns the way those daredevils do. How's our dinner coming along?"

"It should be ready in about ten minutes."

"Good. Why don't you take a shower and slip into something more comfortable?"

He obviously had taken his own advice, because stray drops of water glistened in his short, dark hair as well as on his freshly-shaven cheeks. And he'd put on soft navy blue sweats grayed out from many washings. Those sweats almost exactly matched the color of his eyes.

"Don't you ever wear pajamas?" she asked.

He grinned. "Don't own any. It's this or skin. Your choice."

"It would serve you right if I said skin. It's getting chilly."

"I trust you'll warm me up, soon enough. Go on, do what you need to do, and slip into that sexy nightie Lynn told Mark you two picked out to torture me on our wedding night."

"She told Mark?"

He grinned. "Yeah. And he told me. Good wives tell their husbands everything."

Shelly doubted that, but she didn't say so. Instead, she showered, toweled herself dry, stepped into the tiny lace thong bikini, and slipped on her transparent peach nightgown.

A woman she didn't recognize stared back at her from the full-length mirror. A woman with tousled reddish-brown curls like hers. The woman had a face like hers, yet she was different.

She stared back at an alluring woman who could blow Kurt Silverman's mind.

A woman who was sex personified.

Who was she kidding? She was just Shelly, Kurt's good buddy. It made no difference how she wrapped the package.

Still, she looked okay. Better, she thought when she shrugged into the matching silk robe and belted it securely beneath her breasts. She wasn't cut out to be a sex kitten.

As she stepped out of the bedroom, the timer went off. Shelly shoved food around on her plate while she watched Kurt devour the tangy chicken as greedily as he consumed her with his gaze.

When he set down his fork he said, "Well, brand-new wife of mine, do you want to talk about what we're going to do, or shall we just get on with doing it?"

Her breath caught in her throat. Her pulse raced.

Was she scared or eager?

Both. But she remembered feeling his—his cock, hard and pulsing in her hand, and she realized the wanting was stronger than the fear.

"Let's just do it."

A sexy grin on his face, he scooped her up in his arms and headed for the bedroom.

Chapter Six

Wrapped in peach-colored silk and ivory lace, Shelly reminded Kurt of a long-ago present from his nana that he'd had to look at and yearn for while it sat on the mantel, yet not touch until the time came for unwrapping.

The familiar smell of her flowery cologne reminded him this gorgeous creature was no stranger, just his good friend Shelly.

But holding her felt right. Her silky skin and soft, full lips made him want to consume her in one quick, satisfying bite.

He set her down beside the bed and unhooked the belt that held her robe together, eager to get a good look at the practically transparent silk that had tantalized him while they ate.

The robe parted, then slid to the floor when she shrugged it off her shoulders.

"Oh my God."

Desire slammed into him as though he hadn't jerked off in the shower less than an hour earlier. How could it not when he was standing next to a bed, gaping at a gorgeous woman veiled in illusions except for scraps of lace that drew his attention to her breasts and pussy?

A shy seductress whose smile hinted that she knew what seeing her like this was doing to him, while her trembling lower lip reminded him she was heading into new and scary territory.

Slow. He had to go slow.

A slow touch. Slow, sensual kisses.

He stroked her, his thumbs making lazy circles on her satiny cheeks, his fingers barely making contact as he moved lower and caressed her breasts, her slender waist, the firm curves of her belly and hips.

He trembled like an untried schoolboy. Wanted her now. No. Had to hold back, give her time to catch up.

When she slid her hands under his sweatshirt and exerted gentle pressure at his waist to bring him closer, he nearly lost it.

"Easy there, Shel. You have no idea how close I am already." Close to tumbling her backward onto that bed, spreading her legs and taking her like an animal. "We need to take this slow."

"Why?"

"Because I want you to enjoy it, too."

"I am. Would you take those clothes off? I feel naked compared to you."

Maybe the cool evening air would slow down his eager cock. He snatched the shirt over his head, then shed his pants. So much for his theory about cold air dampening his libido. Kurt made himself stand there, shivering, while blood kept rushing to his cock, getting him harder and hotter by the second. Damn. He had to hold on to some measure of control.

She reached out, brushed her fingers against the tip of his cock, then lay across the bed. "Come here," she said, arms outstretched.

If he didn't pick up the pace, he'd never last long enough to make it good for her. Lying on his side next to her, he gathered a handful of her nightgown and eased it up and over her head.

"How is it I never noticed until a few days ago how beautiful you are?"

Her firm, creamy breasts nestled comfortably in his hands. He bent and suckled one hardened nipple, then the other.

"Ooh. Don't stop. Would it feel good if I did that to you?" She found his nipple, circled it with a finger.

"Yeah." His nipples had never been particularly sensitive, so better that she play with them than with his cock and balls, where her attention would make him explode.

He resumed suckling her, torturing himself with mental pictures of her beautiful breasts swollen with milk to nourish the child he'd promised to give her. His child.

Unlike Adrianna, Shelly would want to nurse their baby. He knew instinctively, though they hadn't talked about it. He sucked harder, his own arousal heightened when she threaded her fingers through his hair and held him to her breast.

He moved one hand lower, toyed with the lace thong that barely hid her pussy. "May I take this off?" he asked after giving her nipple a gentle bite.

"Um-huh." She lifted her hips to give him room, and when he got rid of the scrap of fabric, he cupped her silky mound, insinuated a finger between her warm moist outer lips.

Her clit pulsated when he put gentle pressure on it. As if the sensation frightened her, she closed her legs against his hand.

"Open up for me, Shel."

"It feels—"

"Hot? Exciting?" He moved his finger against her clit again, this time in a circular motion. At the same time he flailed her nipple with his tongue.

She moved her legs again, gave him the room he needed. "It feels like something's going to happen inside of me. Like I'm going to burst. Oh God. Yesss."

He let up on the pressure. She arched her hips as though to maintain the contact, groaned. Her responsiveness to his first intimate touch fed his own need, sent a new surge of blood to his already-engorged cock.

He'd die if he didn't get inside her now. With one knee, he nudged her legs farther apart. Bracing himself on one elbow, he used the other hand to guide his cock to her wet, swollen sex. Then he paused.

"How do you want it, Shel?"

Her eyelids fluttered before she met his gaze. "What?"

Hell, he should have insisted that they talk about this first. Before his cock had taken over for his brain. "The first time for a woman can hurt. I can go slow, stretch you a little at a time, as painlessly as I can. At least I can try. Baby, you've got me damn near mindless with wanting you."

"What's the other choice?"

"I can do it all at once, then stop until you get used to the feel of me inside you. If I can stop, that is. I can't guarantee that I can. Your call."

She reached up, brushed a strand of hair off his forehead. "Just do it, Kurt. Fast. I want you inside me now."

"Okay. Wrap your legs around my waist and hold on."

His cock was hot and hard and so huge that Shelly thought when he entered her in one powerful thrust that she'd split apart. Though she tried, she wasn't able to hold back a tiny yelp of pain.

He held himself rigid above her. The effort it must have cost him to give her time to recover showed in the taut lines around his mouth, the straining muscles in his neck and chest.

"God, Shel, I'm sorry." Balancing himself on one elbow, he cupped her chin, wiped a tear as it slid down her cheek.

"I'm okay."

The searing pain had dulled, and in its place a warm, tingling feeling came over her, settling deep in her belly. Tentatively she tightened her legs around his waist and flexed her hips. The sensation intensified.

She clutched his bulging biceps. Hard, sculpted, yet velvety smooth to her touch, they were damp with a fine layer of sweat. His chest hair tickled her nipples, and his well-developed abs rippled against her as he began to move.

Slowly. Carefully. But his ragged breathing hinted at what his restraint was costing him.

"Fuck me, Shel. Now. So hot. So tight. Can't—can't wait much longer."

Striving for nirvana she sensed lay just beyond her reach, she clung to him, dug her fingers into the straining muscles she'd massaged a hundred times before.

It was incredibly erotic, the slapping sounds of damp flesh coming together. Accompaniment for the delicious friction of him, moving inside her, stretching and filling her. She'd never felt so alive before, never realized...

Their slick bodies skin-to-skin, the tastes and smells and sounds of sex surrounded her. "Don't hold back," she whispered, the pain forgotten with her body's promise of incredible pleasure.

She lifted her hips to meet his next thrust, took him deep and hard. The pressure built as they moved in unison, harder and faster. Tense muscles strained. Beyond thinking, she nipped his shoulder, tasted the salt of his sweat.

"Sorry, baby. Gotta come."

He buried himself deep inside her, so deep he touched the mouth of her womb, and shards of the most incredible pleasure she'd ever known shot through her body, left her drained.

The only thing missing from the equation was love. Shelly told herself as she lay cradled in Kurt's arms that the relationship they had was safer.

Friendship. And a pact to do each other a mutual favor.

* * * * *

The next morning Kurt woke early, stretched. Strange, the silence that reigned instead of traffic sounds from the street below his bedroom window.

When he listened more carefully he heard the sound of water dripping, smelled coffee brewing.

He blinked, then opened his eyes and looked out the window. The sun peeked through a curtain of green, oriented him to his surroundings.

George's cabin on Hope Mountain. Shelly. His bride. His good buddy who'd blown his mind last night with her eager response in bed.

The friend who'd changed overnight from little-sister cute to full-blown gorgeous.

Wide-awake now and getting hard just thinking about last night, Kurt pulled on his sweat pants and followed his nose toward the coffeepot. He pictured Shelly, half asleep and looking good enough to eat in that see-through nightgown he'd taken off her last night.

But it was his buddy Shelly standing at the kitchen counter, covered head to toe in forest green sweats. Only her swollen lips and messed up, reddish-brown curls hinted that she'd just gotten out of bed with her lover.

"Good morning."

She shot him a nervous-looking smile when she looked up from whatever it was she was mixing in a huge pink plastic bowl. "Pancakes okay?"

"Sounds good."

He wanted to kiss her. But part of him held back. He'd never kissed his good pal Shelly when she cooked for him at her place or his. So he settled for brushing his lips across her cheek.

"Eggs?"

"No thanks. Unless you want some."

Kurt poured himself some coffee and sat at the table watching Shelly cook.

What the hell was wrong with him? And what was up with her? Why were they tiptoeing around each other like wary strangers?

They were friends. Good friends. Lovers, too, now. Damn good lovers, too, at least from his perspective.

But he'd hurt her last night with that first hard thrust. "Are you okay?"

"Sure. Why wouldn't I be?"

Her reply was too quick, her voice too bright.

"It was your first time. By the way, I suppose I should thank you for that. It means a lot to know you chose me to be your first lover."

"You're welcome. And you made it good for me, too." She looked down, her cheeks bright pink. "Really good. But I knew you'd be as good at that as you are at everything else."

"I'll get better with repetition, and that's a promise. Before last night, it had been a long time."

She slid a plate full of pancakes in front of him, but he caught her shy smile, guessed his implication that he'd been choosy about sex partners pleased her.

He caught her hand. "How do you really feel, Shel?"

"Fine. You didn't hurt me. It was…unbelievably good, beyond my wildest dreams." When she grinned, he knew his pal Shelly was back. "Better than I've read about in all those romance novels you tease me about reading."

"Good. Still it stands to reason that you'd be a little tender this morning."

Her blush deepened. "A little. But it's nothing."

"Nothing except a good reason that we need to spend the day doing some leisurely sightseeing instead of hiking or replaying last night's activities. What say we drive down the mountain and see what kinds of souvenirs we can find?"

"All right."

They lingered over coffee on the open deck of the cabin and looked for wildlife on the mountain that was just beginning to show signs of the approaching summer.

Kurt found himself watching Shelly, half wanting to take her in his arms while the other half of him reminded him she was his pal, not the love of his life. For the sake of his sanity, he'd better remember that.

Sex. It was just a fringe benefit, not the reason for them being here now, married to each other. A fringe benefit he intended to enjoy fully, though he was beginning to think it was going to take some effort to keep in mind the true reasons he and Shelly had joined forces.

"You said yesterday that you'd need to call and check on a patient this morning," Shelly called to him when he went to the bedroom to get his wallet.

When was the last time his patients had slipped his mind?

Kurt couldn't remember, and the fact that he'd thought nothing of them this morning sealed his resolve to keep thinking of his marriage as a sexually satisfying arrangement between friends, nothing more.

"Thanks. I'll call now," he said, picking up his cell phone and dialing his office number.

* * * * *

Pleasantly exhausted that evening after a day's sightseeing in Gatlinburg, Kurt started a fire and stretched out on the long couch in front of the fireplace, his head on Shelly's lap. Her light floral scent mingled with the pungent smell of the wood fire. A fire whose flames reminded him how silky her soft gingery curls had felt last night when he tangled his fingers in them…and later when they'd cushioned his balls.

She'd been incredibly responsive—so sexy he'd almost forgotten last night had been her first time.

So sexy he'd devoured her as though he'd been starving. Tonight he'd take her slow and easy—drive her crazy. Coax out all the passion he'd been so pleasantly surprised to find beneath Shelly's calm, matter-of-fact manner.

He turned his head, nuzzled her firm, flat belly through her robe and—he guessed—that unbelievably sexy nightie she'd had on last night.

Good thing he was lying down, because the rush of blood to his cock left his head feeling fuzzy. Kurt had the feeling going slow would take some doing.

She brushed her fingers along his jawbone. That sent another surge of blood to his cock. When she slid her hand lower, stroking down his bare chest, that got him hard as stone.

What the fuck had happened to his good buddy who'd been able to lay her healing hands all over his practically naked body without sending his libido into a state of high alert?

Kurt didn't know, and at the moment he didn't care. He wanted to bury his cock inside his good friend Shelly and put out the fire that had him mindless.

Shelly loved the nearness, the curl of heat that started low in her belly where Kurt's warm breath tickled her through the layers of her nightie and robe. Loved soaking in the ambience of the fire on a cool night, watching the shadows shift against the coppery expanse of his muscular chest.

His sweatpants rode low, baring his navel and outlining his sex beneath the dark green fabric. His aroused sex. His cock, she thought, liking the intimacy implied in the stark Anglo-Saxon word—a word she'd never have thought, much less said, before last night.

The forbidden word conjured up erotic thoughts…thoughts of his big, throbbing cock glistening at the tip with sweet-salty lubrication, inviting her to taste it. His demanding cock pushing into her pussy, filling her with its pulsing heat.

She slid her hand lower, curled her fist around him. So hot. So big and hard. The pounding of his pulse made her fingers tingle, her heart beat faster.

Knowing he wanted her set her own pulse to racing.

Burning wood crackled in the fireplace, setting off a shower of sparks that lit Kurt's face, illuminating the pulsing vein in his neck and the hot, needy look in eyes darkened with tightly leashed desire. He skimmed her belly with his fingertips, then sat up enough to nuzzle her breasts.

"You're playing with fire, Shel," he warned her when she gave his cock a tentative squeeze. It swelled more, pressing against her hand as though telling her it was ready to jump into the flame.

She squeezed him again, then angled her body around enough that she could reach the drawstring that held his sweats up. "I'm already burning up," she said when she finally got the knot undone and shoved his sweats down. "And wet. You're wet, too."

"Wanting you, baby. Wanting you bad."

The tortured sound of his voice gave her courage to bend and taste the glistening drop of liquid nestled like a pearl at the tip of his beautiful blue-veined cock. Ravenous, she cupped his balls in her hand and sampled his velvety length with her tongue.

Unbelievably silky and smooth. Satiny. And pulsing with life. Shelly stroked his sac, felt his balls draw up closer to his body when she sucked the head of his cock into her mouth and swirled her tongue around the ridge where it met his long, thick shaft.

He tasted good. Slick and slightly salty. Like the clean, aroused male he was.

"Turn about's fair play," Kurt growled, shifting enough so he could bare her pussy. With his teeth he pulled her lacy thong out of the way. Then he sucked her clit into his mouth and nipped it with his teeth.

What a decadent picture they'd make if anyone were looking, Shelly thought as she sucked his cock deeper down her throat while he licked and nibbled her pussy.

She reached down with one hand, tangled her fingers in his soft, dark hair—hair that tickled her inner thighs while he sent amazing sensations coursing through her with every swipe of his tongue.

Slow. Torturous. Every move he made, each tightening of well-developed muscles, every pulsation of his rock-hard cock inside her mouth fed a need fueled by what he was doing to her pussy.

Pressure built deep in her belly, made her tremble. Made her suck him harder, as if she could devour him the way he was...

God. Her pussy rained its juices and he lapped them up. He snaked his tongue inside her, set off a starburst of sensations that left her panting, then drained. Like when she'd brought herself to climax, only ten times more intense, she thought when he dragged her off his cock and had her straddle his lean, muscular hips.

"Fuck me, baby. Take as much of me as feels good."

Her pulse still pounded in her pussy, or was that the reverberation of his throbbing cock poised at the entrance to her womb? "Oh, Kurt," she murmured as she lowered herself inch by inch onto him, mating their bodies.

He stretched her almost to the point of pain. But it felt good. Full. She wanted more. Wanted him in her so deep she couldn't tell where she ended and he began.

The tips of his fingers had her burning everywhere they touched. Her buttocks and belly. Her clit when he circled it, massaged the aching nub. Her breasts, straining for more contact when he cupped them in his big, gentle hands and lightly pinched the nipples.

Tentatively, she moved on him. Up and down, taking him deeper with every slow rise and fall of her hips. When he joined their mouths she tasted herself on his tongue and lips, the mingled tastes and smells all the aphrodisiac she needed.

Kurt's powerful thigh muscles tightened. His tongue swept the inside of her mouth, and his fingers tightened on her nipples. He strained upward as his cock seemed to swell against the walls of her vagina.

As a log crackled and split apart in the fire, he threw back his head and shouted her name as he began to spurt wave after wave of hot, wet semen inside her. This time her climax began as a warm, full sensation before bursting into flame, spreading out of control through every cell of her body, and leaving her limp and breathless, her head lolling against his still-heaving chest.

* * * * *

For the rest of their days on Hope Mountain, Kurt took care to treat Shelly as the good pal she'd been to him since their first meeting nearly two years earlier.

At night, though, they made slow, sweet love. Kurt couldn't dismiss it as only sex, no matter how hard he tried. Somehow his buddy had gotten to him. Enchanted him with her sweet, hot pussy and bewitched him with her eagerness to please him and take pleasure every time they fucked.

He told himself he'd get his mind right, as soon as they got home and he got back to work.

* * * * *

Soon after they got back to San Antonio, Shelly realized Kurt hadn't been kidding when he'd said she wouldn't have time to work full-time. They'd close on the house today, but she already had spent nearly a week buying furniture—only the bare essentials they'd need right away. She'd have to get a lot more before the place would look and feel like a home.

Meanwhile they'd camped in her apartment, though she doubted Kurt had gotten much rest with his feet hanging off the end of her double bed every night. Hugging the edge of the mattress to keep from sliding off hadn't been too comfortable for her, either.

With luck, the furniture company would have delivered the master bedroom set she'd picked out by the time they finished signing the papers. Shelly's cheeks heated when she thought about them initiating the king-size bed tonight.

That is, if Kurt ever got here. She glanced at the door that opened into his lawyer's private office before glancing again at her watch.

Four-fifteen. He was already fifteen minutes late.

Her pulse raced when he hurried in a few minutes later, looking tired but sexy as sin in the wrinkled lab coat he wore over OR scrubs.

He bent and brushed his lips across her cheek. "Sorry I'm late, Shel. Case took longer than I expected."

Then he turned to Cal. "Have you got the paperwork?"

"Here. Everything's in order. Since you were both coming today, I also drafted the motion to modify the custody arrangement. I'll file it on Monday. Pages where you need to sign have the tabs attached."

Shelly watched Kurt scrawl his name on each marked page.

"Here," he said, handing her the folder. "You need to sign them, too."

Michelle Silverman. She wasn't used to her new name yet. Sometimes she wondered if she shouldn't have been modern and kept her own, especially when she considered the nature of their arrangement.

Still, Shelly couldn't help the small thrill that came over her as she signed the papers.

It shouldn't be such a big deal. After all, she reminded herself, they were married. She slept in Kurt's arms each night after they made the hottest, sweetest love she could imagine.

Dwelling on the reasons they were together like this would spoil her happiness, and that wouldn't do.

She finished signing and passed the folder back to Cal. "All done. Should we plan to have Jason with us soon?"

"There will have to be another hearing, but with luck, Jason will be spending the last half of the summer with you two." After Cal checked the signatures, he looked up and smiled. "Congratulations, Dr. and Mrs. Silverman. You've bought yourselves a house. And you should have your son with you before too long."

Kurt stood, held out his hand to Shelly. "Thanks," he said. "We should have everything ready for him by the middle of June."

That would be cutting it close. Seven weeks or so to turn an empty house into a home.

Shelly would manage it, though. After all, providing a suitable home for his son to visit was the main reason Kurt had married her—the only reason, if she was going to be totally honest with herself.

Chapter Seven

Glad for the free time created when a patient didn't show for his appointment a few days later, Kurt leaned back in the swivel chair behind his desk and studied a framed photo of Shelly, his favorite of many he'd taken of her on Hope Mountain. The sun had caught the coppery highlights in her hair and enhanced the healthy glow on her cheeks.

He'd been right to marry her, though it was getting harder every day to remember the arrangement had everything to do with friendship and not a hint of romantic love.

More likely it was the sex that kept her always on his mind. He'd obviously been celibate too long before they married.

Otherwise he wouldn't ache to get home to his good pal. He wouldn't curse when he got an emergency call that dragged him out of her arms. And his cock certainly wouldn't get hard the way it was now, just looking at her picture.

Yeah, that was it. He was enjoying a sexual feast after a long famine. Understandable.

"Dr. Silverman. Mrs. Silverman is on line three for you," one of the receptionists announced over the intercom.

What he couldn't understand was the way he couldn't wait to hear her voice.

Kurt turned on the speakerphone. "Hi, Shel."

"Surprise, sugar."

God help him. He'd recognize that syrupy drawl anywhere. "Adrianna. What do you want? And why aren't we communicating through our respective attorneys the way we always do?"

"I wanted to congratulate you, of course. And to send condolences to the poor woman you talked into becoming the second Mrs. Silverman. It would be horribly bad form for me not to convey my good wishes in person."

The hairs prickled on the back of Kurt's neck. "That's never stopped you before. Cut to the chase and tell me what you want."

"I just put Jason on a plane. He'll be arriving at the San Antonio airport this afternoon at six-forty." She rattled off the flight information faster than Kurt could write it down.

Kurt swore softly. Leave it to Adrianna to catch him off-guard. "So what brought about the sudden decision to let our son spend an unscheduled weekend with me?" he asked, mentally rearranging his schedule and wondering when he'd find time to prepare the presentation he had to make in Dallas the following weekend.

"The fact that I'm assuming your bride will prove a more responsible babysitter than the housekeepers you've hired. By the way, Jason won't be staying for just a weekend. He's staying two weeks."

"What about school?"

"Your son got himself suspended for the rest of the school year yesterday. Maybe if you can drag yourself away from your precious practice long enough, you can teach him fighting doesn't solve a body's problems."

Kurt clutched the edge of the desk, wrestled his temper under control. He hadn't taught Jason to fight. Couldn't have if he'd wanted to, as little time as Adrianna let him have with his son.

"You're supposed to let me know immediately when something like this happens. Why didn't you?" he asked through clenched teeth.

"I'm letting you know now, sugar. Since you're going back to court to try to get joint custody, I thought you'd be happy to have him come now to stay with you and…what's her name?"

"Shelly."

"I'm sure Shelly will love getting the chance to meet her stepson before you two have to fight me in court. Incidentally, Jason's not at his best right now. He's terribly upset about missing the Little League playoff games."

"Why?" Kurt couldn't imagine Jason voluntarily missing those games. If there was one thing the kid loved, it was playing baseball.

"Because the coach said he deliberately hit a little boy on another team with a baseball."

Kurt couldn't help thinking the last round of custody hearings had a lot to do with this hostile behavior. Guilt stung him, fueled his fury.

"I'm sure the fact he's not at his best, as you say, has nothing to do with your decision to send him to me now," he said, not even trying to mask his sarcasm.

"Why of course it does. I told him he's spending two weeks with you to remind him not to act like a little savage."

Kurt imagined Adrianna smiling, her glittering gaze full of venom. "Damn you."

It hurt to hear that spending time with him was punishment for Jason. Kurt propped his elbows on his desk and rested his aching head on outstretched hands.

"Wait a minute, sweetie. There's another reason I'm sending Jason to you. He broke two toes a couple of months ago, and they haven't healed right. Since you live and breathe bones, I figure you can see to having whatever needs doing, done, and make sure he's healing properly before you send him home."

"Why didn't I hear about this when it happened?"

"I told my attorney. He was going to tell yours." From Adrianna's bored tone, Kurt imagined she'd just given her shoulders an elegant little shrug.

"Get his doctor to send me the records." Asking her to expand on the nature of their son's injury would be futile.

"I already have. They're being faxed to your office today. I wouldn't be surprised if they were already there."

"All right, Adrianna. Shelly or I will pick Jason up at the airport. Give me the flight number again."

He filled in the blanks on the scribbled numbers he'd jotted down when Adrianna first called, then glanced at the clock. Only two hours until Jason was due to arrive.

"I guess I should thank you for letting me know he was coming in time for me to meet his flight," he said, making no effort to veil his sarcasm.

"You're welcome. I told Jason to call you if no one showed up to collect him, so there's no need for you to drag yourself out of the hospital if you don't feel like it. After all, he doesn't expect a whole lot of attention from you."

Kurt stifled the crude comment that came to mind. Likely as not, Adrianna would use lapses in his language as another weapon in their ongoing war.

"Save it for the courtroom, Adrianna. You know damn well I won't leave my son stranded at the airport. Incidentally, you might want to give serious thought to how you're going to explain to the judge why you didn't tell me about Jason's injury—and why you're poisoning his mind against me by using visits here as punishment."

"Whatever, as Jason would say. It sounds as though you've used up your limited supply of civility, so I'll let you go. 'Bye, and good luck."

Kurt thought he heard his ex-wife laugh before the phone went dead.

He had no illusions. This visit was to be his test. If it worked out, he'd have a good chance to win his bid for joint custody. If not…

Adrianna had better pray no complications arose from delaying treatment for Jason's injury.

Willing away the pounding at his temples, Kurt called Shelly, told her Jason was coming, and arranged to meet her at the airport. Then he strode to the fax machine.

Good. Jason's records were here.

On the way back to his office he skimmed the ER report. The original injury wasn't quite as simple as Adrianna had claimed. Nondisplaced fractures to two metatarsals and the large and middle phalanxes had to have taken some doing.

According to the record, the fractures had happened when Jason kicked the base of the entertainment center in his room. Kurt sat at his desk and read the rest of the reports, idly wondering how the piece of furniture had fared. Apparently the ER doc had opted to tape the foot to immobilize it since the fractures were incomplete, but Jason had failed to stay off his foot long enough to heal. He had, instead, exacerbated the original injuries.

Kurt would have put Jason in a cast at the outset, considering the boy's obviously hot temper.

And it appeared he'd have been right. Unless he was mistaken, his son would now need open surgery to repair the additional damage he'd inflicted.

Meanwhile he'd never be able to get to the airport before Jason's plane landed unless he left now. Not in afternoon rush hour traffic. He started to shed his lab coat.

The phone rang again, and he snatched it up, one arm still hung up in a sleeve. "Silverman."

A paramedic shouted over the deafening noise of a med-evac helicopter's engines.

They were ten minutes away from University Hospital with a rancher who'd been gored by a bull near Fredericksburg.

Kurt strained to hear. Multiple fractures. Horn had nicked a femoral artery. Patient bleeding out. Going straight to the OR.

"I'm on my way."

Jason. Shelly would have to get him by herself.

While jogging from his office to the hospital across the street, he called her.

"Don't worry, I'll get him. Go take care of that poor rancher. Jason and I will get along fine."

As Kurt changed and scrubbed, Shelly's words echoed in his head.

Thank God she was nothing like Adrianna.

* * * * *

Jason's flight was late. Shelly paced the waiting area, wishing she'd had more time to prepare her stepson's room before his visit. Why had Kurt had to get called in for an emergency case tonight?

She stopped in front of a glass-enclosed advertising poster and finger-combed her hair, then glanced at her reflection in the makeshift mirror.

The dark slacks and white tunic she hadn't taken time to change out of after working this morning looked institutional. Boring. At least she thought so, and she imagined Kurt's son would see her that way, too. When she compared herself the way she looked today with the photo of Jason's beautiful blond, put-together mother that she'd set on the brand-new dresser in his room, Shelly came up way short.

Who was she kidding? She'd come up way short even if she were at her best.

Shelly had figured she would, before unpacking the box of Jason's things from his old room at Kurt's apartment and coming across Adrianna's picture. Seeing it had confirmed her hunch that the woman was gorgeous.

"Flight 642 has landed. Passengers will unload at gate A-sixteen."

Along with a few dozen others, Shelly crowded as close as she could to the turnstile the arriving passengers would come through. She imagined she'd recognize Jason from the pictures Kurt had shown her, and she did. A flight attendant escorted the angry-looking boy down the aisle from the gate.

Shelly stepped forward. "Jason?"

"Who are you, and where's my dad?"

"I'm Shelly, your dad's wife. He would have come, but he had an emergency case."

Jason's only response was silence. Sullen silence punctuated by an even darker scowl that distorted his features.

Shelly imagined Jason smiling. He looked a lot like Kurt, except for lighter coloring and the china-blue eyes he must have gotten from his mother.

"Jason, is this your stepmother?" the flight attendant asked.

Jason shrugged. "Probably. I never met her, but it sounds like she knows my dad. All he does is hang around hospitals cuttin' on people."

Shelly dug in her purse, pulled out her driver's license and a couple of credit cards that had Kurt's name on them. "I'm Michelle Silverman. Jason and I haven't met before. Here's some identification."

The flight attendant looked, then smiled at Jason. "Thank you for flying with us today, Jason. Enjoy your visit to San Antonio."

The attendant's smile lacked a certain degree of sincerity.

"Shall we go get your bags?" Shelly asked.

Jason shrugged, but followed along when she headed to the baggage pickup area. Despite other travelers talking all around them, Shelly found her stepson's silence deafening.

"How was your flight?" she asked when she managed to insinuate herself between two tall men and stand beside

Jason in the front row of passengers waiting at the baggage carousel.

As though he found the flashing "Flight 642" sign above the carousel a whole lot more interesting than conversation, Jason didn't even glance her way.

"Boring," he muttered just as Shelly was beginning to wonder if he had a hearing problem.

Again, silence. But luggage started going around the carousel. Maybe when they got home, the boy would open up a little.

"What does your luggage look like?"

"I don't know. Mom packed it." He handed over his ticket folder with two baggage claim checks attached.

Great. Why did Shelly not believe Jason had no idea what his own suitcases looked like? Could it be the surly smirk on his face as she strained to see the numbers on each unclaimed bag that rolled by?

Finally she spotted them. Two huge navy duffel bags, both with distinctive brand name logos in bright white and emerald green. Shelly dragged them off the carousel and turned to Jason.

"Is that all?"

"Yeah. How're you gonna carry them?"

He looked strong enough to manage one, but Shelly kept that thought to herself.

"We'll get a skycap." She waved at one who seemed to be looking for a customer.

"I guess you'll have to, since Dad managed to find something else to do tonight."

"Your father was called back to do emergency surgery. It isn't as though he didn't want to be here to meet you."

Shelly had the feeling she was wasting her breath, a feeling that strengthened when Jason's only response was another elaborate shrug. The boy needed some lessons in manners. But now wasn't the time or place, and she probably wasn't the right person to give them.

She shifted her gaze, noticed that he limped. "Did you hurt yourself?"

"Yeah. That's why Mom sent me here, so Dad can get my toes fixed. They hurt like crazy. Mom gave me a pill before I left Atlanta, but that was nearly three hours ago."

Shelly opened the passenger door of the sport utility vehicle Kurt had insisted on buying for her. "Okay. Hop in."

"I want to call my mom," he said the minute she started the car.

She handed him her cell phone, listened as he talked to someone who obviously was not his mother. She sighed. Kurt hadn't told her his son was a full-blown problem child.

But then it wouldn't have mattered. She'd still have married him if he'd told her she'd be helping him take care of a monster.

"Here." Jason handed her the phone as she pulled onto the divided highway. "What do I call you?"

So he could make small talk after all. "Shelly."

"So why did you marry my dad? Mom says anyone who'd marry him has got to be crazy."

"Hmmm." Shelly had no intention of tackling that one.

Traffic had died down. She turned off the highway, pointed out the two university campuses on either side of the crossroad as she waited for the light to change.

"Dad moved?"

"Yes. We just got the house two weeks ago. Your room's okay, but some of the downstairs still looks bare."

"You got a pool?"

"Uh-huh. And a weight room. Your dad will have to show you how to use the equipment there, though."

"Like that'll happen."

"Jason, your father loves you." *So much he married me just to make a home for you.*

He laughed as she pulled into the garage next to Kurt's classic Alfa. "Sure he does. Only thing my dad loves is the rush he gets, saving people's lives. You gotta go pick him up at the hospital?"

"No. He has his other car today."

"What other car?"

"A Mercedes sports car. I don't remember the model."

Jason got out, squinted into the backyard floodlights that lit the pool and house. "Killer. What color is it?"

"Black. Think you can carry one of these bags?"

"Can't the maid do it?" he asked, that sullen look firmly back in place now.

God, how did this kid's mother live? "We don't have live-in help. I'm afraid the toting's up to you and me. Grab that bag. I'll get the other one."

One constant battle with no let-up. That's how Shelly felt after two hours with a recalcitrant, surly child too big to banish to a corner. An angry kid who wasn't about to let go of his anger and try to have fun. She sat at the kitchen table and looked out at the sparkling pool after Jason finally went upstairs to bed.

At least he'd said the house beat Kurt's old apartment, but that was faint praise, considering she'd seen those plain vanilla rooms. The institutional-looking rented furniture had blended into tan carpeting that looked as if it had been chosen for no other reason than that it didn't show dirt. And Jason had shown a smidgeon of interest in the pool that was, he observed, smaller than the one he had at home.

A boy that young shouldn't be so angry. Shelly closed her eyes, tried to imagine what she could do to help make Jason happy while he was here.

When she heard the distinctive roar of Kurt's car in the drive, she glanced at the clock on the microwave. Twelve-thirty. He'd be exhausted, too tired to think about anything except food and sleep—maybe not even food.

Still she went to the refrigerator, set out cold meats, cheese, tossed salad, and some fresh raspberries she'd found at the store this afternoon. If he didn't want to eat, she could always put the food away.

"Hi. Are you too tired to eat?" she asked when he walked through the door, still in OR scrubs, a paper mask dangling around his neck.

"No. I'm starved. Did Jason get here all right?"

"Yes. He went to bed about ten. Kurt, he's not a happy child—"

"Not now, Shel. I'm already mad enough at Adrianna to chew nails. And too damn exhausted to trust myself to hold onto my temper. Wait 'til morning to give me more bad news about my son. What I'd appreciate now is a back rub."

That she could do. Moving behind him, Shelly kneaded the knotted muscles of his upper arms and shoulders while he ate.

Chapter Eight

"Don't say a word. Just keep on touching me the way you were doing downstairs. Please."

Tonight Kurt didn't get the sense of peace and homecoming he usually found when he shed his clothes and crawled onto the goose down feather mattress Shelly had found for their bed. Hammers pounded in his head, punctuating the rhythm of the throbbing muscles in his neck and shoulders.

He rolled onto his belly and made a conscious effort to shed the helpless fury that had gripped him when he looked at Jason's medical record and realized his son might end up permanently impaired.

When cool lotion met his heated skin, he stifled a protest. Then Shelly started working her magic again. Her hands, strong yet gentle on his naked skin, kneaded away the tension as well as a soreness that had as much to do with his anger as with the effort he'd expended, trying to save that rancher's leg.

"Feels great. Don't stop."

"If I didn't know better, I'd think you married me to get massages every night," Shelly commented, but she kept up the rhythmic motion on his back and shoulders.

Her firm inner thighs warmed his legs where she straddled him, and his cock stirred in spite of his exhaustion. Suddenly guilt hit Kurt.

Shelly had to be tired, too, and stressed from having had to deal with his son for the first time, alone. He'd noticed the dark circles under her eyes in the kitchen earlier. But she hadn't uttered a word of protest when he'd asked her for a backrub.

"Feels great, but that's enough for now." Reaching back, he caught one of her hands and squeezed.

When she slid off him onto her side of the bed, Kurt rolled onto his side and met her gaze. "Thanks for all you did tonight. I don't know how I'd manage without you."

Then he pulled her close and held her. Whatever it took, he'd cut back on work while Jason was here, do his part to keep his son from complicating Shelly's life.

* * * * *

"I hear a full ER moon struck last night," practice administrator Gordon Blake told Kurt the following day after he finished seeing patients in the office. "By the way, I hope your son got here all right."

"He did. I'm glad you stopped by, because I need you to find someone else to make that speech in Dallas next week. I hadn't realized Jason would be here, or I wouldn't have said I'd go."

Gordon shook his head. "Can't do it. I'd send Mark in your place, but he's scheduled to speak there, too. There's no one else."

Kurt had looked forward to taking Shelly with him, repeating the sexual feast they'd enjoyed those first few days on Hope Mountain. Instead, going to the conference now would mean he'd spend two nights alone in a Dallas hotel — or schmoozing at the bar with fellow surgeons who'd be too drunk after a couple of hours to remember their own names, let alone his. He had no desire to go alone.

And he needed to spend time with Jason.

"What about sending someone with another trauma specialty — thoracic surgery?" he asked, grasping at straws now.

"To talk to a convention of orthopedic surgeons? That wouldn't go over at all. Come on, Kurt. You're married now. Don't tell me Shelly can't handle your kid by herself for a couple of days. After all, it's not as though he's likely to get into trouble."

From Adrianna's description of the way Jason had been acting lately, Kurt wasn't too certain about that. He hated asking Shelly to put up with the boy for two hours, let alone two days, if his son's mood when they'd talked for a few minutes over breakfast was typical.

"Cut me some slack. Would you want to stick your bride of less than two months with a surly pre-teen at his worst? A kid who's going to have a cast all the way up to his knee after Mark repairs the bones in his foot on Tuesday?"

"You said you'd go, and you have to do it. There's nobody I can send in your place. Hell, it's not every day a small specialty practice like ours has an opportunity for the kind of free publicity you and Mark will get, talking about how you achieve success with secondary bone, nerve, and tissue reconstruction. You'll attract referrals from all over the southwest."

Referrals that contributed heavily to Kurt's continuing financial security as well as the high quality of applicants to University Hospital's orthopedic residency program. Though Gordon didn't say the words, Kurt heard them.

"All right, Gordon. Forget I asked."

The administrator had him over a barrel. Kurt knew it. Gordon's self-satisfied grin said it all.

Unlike Adrianna, who had complained about everything, Shelly wouldn't say a mean word about him leaving her at home with his troubled son. Kurt doubted she would even think an unkind thought.

He sighed. No wife, especially Shelly, deserved being dumped on. Not when all she did was make his life a hell of a lot more pleasant than it had been before they got married.

Without a doubt, asking her to take care of Jason on her own while he wasn't within shouting distance would be considered dumping by anyone with half a brain.

But damn it, he had no choice. He had a job to do.

He didn't have to stay and work late tonight, however. At least he didn't have to at the moment.

Five minutes later Kurt pulled out of the parking lot into rush hour traffic he seldom encountered. With luck, the full moon demons wouldn't come out in force again the way they had last night. As he made his way through a sea of cars, he tried to figure how he could persuade Shelly they should relax and enjoy each other instead of catering to Jason. As much as he hated that Adrianna had sent his son to him as punishment, he had to admit the boy's attitude could stand adjusting.

Hell, maybe he'd stop at the mall and get Shelly a surprise. God knew, she deserved to be weighed down with diamonds after riding herd on Jason all day long—not to say she didn't already merit all he could give her, just for being his friend and lover.

* * * * *

He was home early, not late, and he came bearing a huge vase full of yellow rosebuds, the edges of their unfurled petals tinged with pale shell pink.

Shelly took them and inhaled their spicy-sweet fragrance. "Thanks. What's the occasion?"

"No occasion. I saw them in the mall and thought you'd like them."

Kurt? At the mall? Before dark on a weekday?

"Thanks." She shut off the vacuum cleaner and brushed a stray curl out of her eyes. The delicious fragrance from the roses swirled around her, enveloped her, made her feel pretty even though she had put on ratty shorts and an old T-shirt to clean up after the furniture delivery people.

Kurt took the vase, set it on the glass-topped dining table that had just been delivered. "I like the table and chairs. Come here."

She stepped into his open arms and tilted her head for his kiss. But he scooped her into his arms instead and carried her upstairs.

"Kurt. Remember, Jason's here."

How the hell could he have forgotten? He set Shelly down beside their bed.

"Guess my horny cock had better ask for a rain check." He dropped a quick kiss on the end of her nose. "Where is he?"

"His room. I think his foot's bothering him. I sneaked a look when he was walking through the kitchen on the way to the pool, and —"

"Damn it, I know all about Jason's foot."

Immediately Kurt regretted snapping at Shelly. It wasn't her fault Adrianna was a bitch. "Sorry. That was out of line."

"It's all right."

"No, it isn't. I've got no business taking out my anger on you. It's frustrating, though."

She smiled. "Of course it is. But Jason is here now. And you can see that he gets whatever medical care he needs."

Kurt clenched his fists. Damn it to hell, Adrianna shouldn't have let Jason re-injure himself. And Jason shouldn't have lost his temper and kicked the entertainment center in the first place.

Jason's anger wasn't Kurt's fault. Thanks to Adrianna, an Atlanta judge had pretty much nudged him out of his son's life. Telephone calls didn't make up for being together.

Of course they hadn't been together all the time when Jason was here, either. And his work was going to interfere again, a niggling voice inside Kurt's head reminded him.

He sat on the edge of the bed and drew Shelly down beside him. Then he let out a sigh.

"Are you okay?" she asked.

"No. I keep telling myself it's not my fault Jason's angry. That Adrianna does nothing to keep him under control. Unfortunately I don't quite believe I'm blameless."

Shelly squeezed his hand. "I think all kids go through a difficult stage."

"I doubt many are as difficult as Jason. According to Adrianna, he didn't pay attention to the doctor when she told him to stay off his foot and keep the broken toes immobilized. From what Mark and I saw in his records, he's going to need open surgery to repair the damage. I'll take him to the office with me on Monday so Mark can take a look, if you can bring him home afterward."

"He'll have surgery here?"

"On Tuesday. Unless Mark decides when he examines Jason that it's not necessary."

"I don't understand. Why did his mother send him here if he needs an operation?"

"So he can benefit from my expertise, or so she said. She also mentioned that this visit is Jason's punishment for getting himself suspended from school for the rest of the school year."

"She couldn't have meant that." Shelly sounded aghast.

When Kurt cupped her chin, she brushed her lips across his palm. So soft. Unlike his former wife, Shelly was soft all over, not just on the outside.

"You couldn't, Shel. But then you aren't Adrianna, for which I thank my lucky stars."

The emotions Shelly evoked scared Kurt half to death. They felt entirely too much like the sort of feelings he'd once had for Adrianna, too much like that deep-down connection that had left him adrift when it was broken.

Kurt wouldn't risk hurting like that again. He let go of Shelly, trying to ignore the feeling of isolation he'd imposed on himself by holding back.

As though Shelly sensed his emotional withdrawal, she lifted her head, stood, and moved over by the French doors that opened onto a balcony. The distance between them was barely five feet, but she couldn't have gone farther had she flown to the other side of the earth.

"Why do you clam up on me, Kurt?" Her voice was tentative, too unsure to be coming from his good friend Shelly.

Denial was at the tip of his tongue, but he owed her the truth. "You're too good to be true," he said, resorting to cliché when his brain wouldn't cooperate and conjure up the right words to express the peace and hope and joy he'd found in her. Or his certainty that those feelings couldn't last.

She laughed, but he read confusion in her troubled gaze.

"You know me, Shel. Good hands, lousy bedside manner. Tell me, what did you and Jason get into today?"

"He likes the pool, and he said my steak fajitas tasted good."

Her report went downhill from there. Jason had spent the better part of the day holed up in his bedroom, music blaring on the boom box, emerging now and then to make snide comments and complain about having to be here. While Shelly gently characterized his son as unhappy and hurting from his own mistreatment of his foot, Kurt wasn't half as generous in his assessment.

He'd thought so before, but now he knew it. Adrianna had spoiled Jason rotten. She'd also poisoned his son's mind against him.

He'd have to work on that, but first the boy needed some serious discipline, and Kurt would have to wield the figurative stick. Pity Adrianna wasn't close enough for him to wield it on her.

"I'll have a talk with Jason."

"Kurt, please. He'll know I told you everything he's said and done since he got here."

He clenched his fists so tight, his fingernails dug into his palms. "I won't have my son making your life miserable. Or playing the poor misunderstood kid from a broken home. This is all Adrianna's doing, damn it."

"Then don't blame Jason. He's just a child."

"He's twelve years old and smart enough to get my drift when I tell him how much more miserable his life can become if he doesn't lose the attitude and mind his manners."

Shaking her head, she moved closer, placed a hand on his chest as if to restrain him. "I don't think fear's the best of motivators."

"Probably not. But I see a problem, I fix it. In this case, I'll tell my son what I expect of him and what he can expect from me if he doesn't deliver. As far as I'm concerned, that's logic, not intimidation."

Shelly shook her head. "I don't think you can fix an unhappy child the way you do a broken leg."

"What do you suggest, a shrink?" Kurt never had put much faith in his colleagues who'd gone into psychiatry. Too much mumbo-jumbo, not enough cold hard facts for his liking.

"N — no."

"Then what, if not some hard-and-fast rules?"

Suddenly she seemed to have developed a great interest in examining her wedding and engagement rings. She wasn't looking at him, that was for sure.

"It's not up to me," she finally said. "I'm sorry if I overstepped myself."

"Damn it, you haven't overstepped anything. You're not only my wife, you're my friend. I respect your opinions on everything else. Why wouldn't I want to hear what you have to say about Jason?"

"He's your son, not mine." She looked him in the eye. "I think, if you really want to know, that he needs a lot of love and attention along with those rules you're planning to set. Seems to me he may not be sure where he stands with you."

That made sense. And Kurt knew he was at least in part to blame. He nodded. "You're probably right. Unfortunately I can't get out of giving that speech in Dallas next weekend, so I'll be reinforcing whatever ideas Adrianna has put into Jason's head about me caring more about my work than I do about him. I'll also be sticking you with a kid who's likely to become even more obnoxious once he's had surgery. And that's not fair to you."

She laughed as she came to him and wrapped her arms around his waist. "I'll survive. There's no reason for you to intimidate Jason into behaving like a robot so he won't offend my tender sensibilities."

"Yeah, there is. But I promise, I'll take it easy on him — easier than he deserves."

She felt good in his arms, and for the moment he let down his defenses and just enjoyed feeling the rhythm of her heart beating against his chest. "I wanted to take you with me, you know. To hibernate in a hotel suite and fuck like minks all weekend except when I'm presenting that paper."

"I'd have liked that. But there'll be other times."

There would be. Kurt would see to it. "Oh, yeah. Lots of times. You're addictive, Shel."

"Really?" She gave his cock a playful squeeze.

"Yeah, really."

"Jason and I will get along okay, I promise. I will miss you, though."

Kurt would miss her, too. A lot, and not just in bed. He was getting himself in too deep. He knew it, but didn't know how to squelch those unwanted emotions. Feelings he doubted he could pass off much longer as nothing more than sexual satisfaction and friendship.

Especially to himself.

Chapter Nine

Whatever Kurt said to Jason the following day when he took the boy with him on hospital rounds seemed to have worked wonders.

Shelly hadn't heard a sarcastic crack since they got home, and if her eyes hadn't deceived her, her stepson actually tried to curl his lips up in a smile a few minutes ago at something Kurt said.

Hopefully Kurt had used reason instead of threats to bring about the apparent change in Jason's attitude.

Looking out the bay window while she made sandwiches, she enjoyed watching father and son tossing a baseball back and forth.

Naked except for boxer-style swim trunks and a fielder's mitt, Kurt stood on the deck and stretched, then tossed the ball back to Jason. Kurt's taut muscles rippled beneath deep golden skin that glistened with drops of water and the residue of tanning oil he'd applied before diving into the pool a few minutes earlier.

Her mouth watered. If she sampled him right now, she'd taste salt and coconut and sexy, sexy man. Then Jason moved into her line of vision, cooling the fantasy.

He could have been Kurt twenty years ago or so. Tall for his age but seemingly all arms and legs, he had a long way to go before he'd match his father's six-three height and two hundred well-muscled pounds.

Still the resemblance amazed Shelly. Maybe her own child would be lucky, too, and inherit Kurt's dark good looks.

She set another turkey and Swiss cheese sandwich on a tray, then touched her flat stomach. Already their baby might be growing there. Part of her hoped so. Another part wanted the process to take longer—months or even years of lying in Kurt's arms each night, enjoying every minute of making that precious part of him and her.

Maybe their lovemaking would go on even if, as she suspected, she was already pregnant. After all, Kurt seemed to enjoy their time in bed as much as she did. And he was as affectionate as ever at other times...maybe more so since they'd become lovers as well as friends.

But he didn't love her the way she loved him. She couldn't delude herself into thinking he did, just because he was applying himself to the task of making her pregnant with the same kind of focus, determination, and dedication he gave to performing operations or completing any other task he undertook.

"Shel?"

She turned away from the window, met Kurt's gaze as he stood framed in the open doorway.

"Have enough sunshine already?" Good thing he couldn't tell what she was thinking.

"No, but I thought I'd grab a couple of sodas for Jason and me. How long until lunch?"

It would have been ready now, if he hadn't inadvertently distracted her with his gorgeous nearly naked self. But that wasn't his fault. "About five minutes," she told him as she started assembling another sandwich.

"Okay. Shall I take out a drink for you, too?"

"A diet cola, please. I'll bring lunch outside. Does Jason like mustard and mayonnaise?"

"I never noticed."

She shouldn't have asked. After all, Kurt hadn't been able to recall what color the paneling in his office was when they'd shopped together for some desk accessories, back when he'd first come to San Antonio. How could she expect him to have noticed which condiments his son used on sandwiches?

"I'll put the extras on the tray, and we can help ourselves."

"That works for me." Kurt gave her bottom a playful squeeze, grabbed three sodas from the refrigerator, and headed back outside.

It amazed Shelly how fast sandwiches went together when one concentrated on making them instead of ogling her husband. In less than a minute, she assembled the last one and stacked small bags of chips, condiments, and silverware on the tray. She brought the simple lunch to the umbrella table beside the pool.

"Hey, this is good," Jason mumbled through a mouthful of food. Then he swallowed and looked Shelly's way. "Did you make dessert?"

"No. But I'll bake some brownies, and we can have them with ice cream. Later, after we go inside."

"O-kay!" he said, grabbing another quarter of a sandwich and shoving it in his mouth. When Jason grinned, Shelly noticed for the first time that he had braces on his teeth.

One honest-to-God open-mouthed smile, and she'd captured it in slightly less than a day. Of course, Shelly told herself while mixing chopped pecans into brownie batter later, it was most likely the prospect of chocolate that had earned that grin.

Jason confirmed her suspicion later when he smiled again, because this time that blissful expression was directed straight toward the hot fudge sundae-topped brownies Shelly set in front of him and Kurt.

* * * * *

"Just feed the kid and he'll be happy," Lynn quipped when Shelly mentioned Jason's healthy appetite on Monday.

Shelly laughed. "I take it you've met Jason before."

It felt good to be back at the office, even though she wasn't on the work schedule and wouldn't be, as long as Jason was with them.

"Mark's taking his time with Jason." Lynn glanced at her watch. "Want to have a quick salad across the street?"

"I'd better not. I'd hate for Jason to have to wait."

Lynn shook her head. "So now you have two demanding males to cater to. I don't believe you. Hasn't anybody ever told you it's the woman who's supposed to lead her man around by the balls?"

"Shel, come on in Mark's office." Kurt's voice boomed over the intercom, making Shelly jump.

"The master calls. Better scurry on to him. Seriously, Shelly, your patients miss you. Hurry back."

When she stepped inside Mark's office, Kurt motioned to the empty spot beside him on a cozy-looking leather sofa.

Jason slumped in the chair opposite Mark's desk, his face a study in rebellion. "Why's she here?" he asked, his tone suddenly as surly as it had been when Shelly picked him up at the airport.

"Because *she's* the one who'll have to ride herd on you the first few days after this surgery. Now be quiet and listen."

Shelly watched Kurt's knuckles turn white when he clenched his fists. His talented hands worked much like a weathervane, she'd noticed — and white knuckles always predicted a nasty storm.

Mark hung the X-rays, then sat behind his desk and explained the operation he'd do to repair Jason's damaged foot and toes. "I'll re-break the metatarsals and pin them back in place. That means you're going to spend six weeks in a cast, longer if you don't follow orders," he said in conclusion.

"You do realize, son, that none of this would be necessary if you'd done what your doctor in Atlanta told you to do the first time?" Kurt got up, stalked to the X-ray viewer, and pointed out the damage Jason had done to himself following the original injury.

"You don't need to rub it in."

Jason shrugged, but Shelly sensed that fear lurked somewhere beyond his look of studied boredom.

When Kurt took his seat, Mark outlined what Jason would and wouldn't be able to do following the operation he had scheduled for tomorrow morning.

She'd need to stop by a bookstore and get the boy some reading material. Maybe some computer games. Jason could use Kurt's laptop while propped up in bed or on the sofa.

Shelly had a feeling she'd be dealing with the world's least cooperative patient—and that Mark's instructions were falling on deaf pre-teen ears.

* * * * *

"My foot hurts. Are you sure Dr. Blackstone knew what he was doing?"

Shelly lifted Jason's leg, re-positioned it on the pillow for the hundredth time in the past three days. "You've got to keep the leg elevated. I'll get you a pain pill in a few minutes."

"When will Dad be back from Dallas?"

"Late tonight."

He stretched, got the phone. Down went his leg, off the pillow and precariously close to the edge of the bed. "I'm calling Mom again," he said, as though daring Shelly to object.

"All right. Let's get your leg back up on those pillows first."

Catering to her stepson was getting old. Shelly's back ached, and her stomach had felt queasy ever since early this morning, when she'd been cooking the bacon Jason had insisted he wanted for breakfast.

So much for the state-of-the-art kitchen exhaust system the realtor told her would instantly get rid of every sort of grease and odor. As she stood over the toilet in the master bathroom, Shelly figured it was a good thing she and Kurt weren't heavily into fried meat. If they were, chances were they'd be eating out a lot for the next eight months or so.

She was pregnant.

Shelly knew it, though she hadn't found the time to use the boxed test she'd picked up at the supermarket before becoming the twenty-four-seven nursemaid to a twelve-year-old tyrant.

"Shelly!"

She hardly had time to throw up. "Coming, Jason," she yelled, willing her nausea to subside.

"Would you mind bringing me a cola?"

Reminding herself he was in pain, she bit back a comment about the half-full glass of iced tea he'd demanded fifteen minutes earlier.

"Okay." She headed back downstairs.

The kitchen exhaust fan still whirred away, and the smell of bacon grease still hung in the air. This time Shelly barely made it into the downstairs powder room before heaving her guts out.

"Hey, you don't look so good," Jason commented when he took the can of cola from her shaky hand a few minutes later and upended it into his mouth.

Shelly tried for a smile. "I'm all right. Do you need anything else?"

"Not now. I'll yell if I do."

That, Shelly had no trouble believing. Jason had proved his willingness to yell for anything that came to mind.

By the time she had him tucked in and sleeping for what she hoped would be the last time for the night, Shelly was exhausted. So exhausted she didn't know whether to fall into bed or scream. Screaming might wake Jason and launch her into another round of cook and fetch and retch, so she chose bed.

* * * * *

Bed. His own bed, complete with his warm, willing best friend Shelly. That's all Kurt had wanted when he exchanged his first class ticket on the late flight home for a middle seat coach spot on an earlier flight.

Sure, he'd known getting his six-three, two-hundred-pound body into that seat would require some serious contortions. But he hadn't realized he'd be wedged like a scrunched up, overgrown sardine between two Sumo wrestlers who'd seriously needed that middle seat as spillover for excess rolls of blubber.

His eyes burned, and hammers pounded at his temples. He hadn't slept well in the big, empty hotel bed. More than once while he was in Dallas, he'd awakened reaching for Shel, seeking her touch, the moisture of her breath against his neck, the welcoming softness of her body next to his.

As he stowed his luggage in the back of his car, he figured the forty-five minutes of torture he'd just endured on that plane was worth it, considering the pleasure that waited for him at home.

* * * * *

The front of the house was dark, but Shelly had left a light on in the kitchen. Kurt pulled into the garage and slid out of the car. His legs protested. His back ached almost enough to make him ignore the insistent throbbing of his cock.

Maybe he should invent a new malady—he could call it coach seat syndrome—and devise some radical treatment to cure it. Possibly he could use it to earn another five minutes of fame, writing a paper on the subject for one of the medical journals. He could get the group some more publicity, presenting it at another conference much like the one he'd just attended.

But he wasn't going to invent it now. At the moment he wanted a cold beer, a shower, and Shelly…not necessarily in that order.

He went for the beer first, though, and when he opened the refrigerator door, he noticed Shelly's note and groaned. His office manager had scheduled him to do surgery at seven the next morning.

A limb salvage on a patient he'd never seen. A teenage girl with osteosarcoma.

Great. Just great. He stared at the note, shaking his head.

Brew in hand, he trudged upstairs. A trickle of light from under Jason's door drew him. He grinned at the sight of his son, headphones in place, sound asleep while the ancient movie playing on TV cast an eerie glow around the otherwise darkened room.

Jason's injured foot rested on a pillow. The exposed tips of his toes looked good, and most of the swelling had gone down. Setting his beer on the nightstand, Kurt took the headphones off Jason's ears.

The boy stirred but didn't awaken when Kurt felt his brow. Satisfied that Jason wasn't feverish, he turned off the TV before heading for his own room.

Shelly was sleeping, too, and Kurt didn't have the heart to wake her, so he made his way through their bedroom in the dark. Once he'd closed the bathroom door he turned on some light, but it wasn't until he set his beer on the counter below the mirror that he noticed the small pink-and-blue box with a picture of a smiling infant on its side.

He picked up the box. Only two of the three test kits remained. The other, he noticed, rested with a couple of crumpled tissues in the bottom of the wastepaper basket.

His gut clenched. Sweat strained to get out through his pores even though the air conditioning was blowing plenty cold.

Yeah, Kurt knew better than the average guy what the usual consequences were for having unprotected sex even once, let alone night after night. And he hadn't forgotten that he and Shelly had gone at it nearly every night since they got married. Or that he'd promised to do his best to make her pregnant as fast as he could.

His knowledge and the discarded test kit led him to a logical conclusion. His very pleasurable efforts had borne fruit quickly. Probably on their honeymoon.

So why did the idea of Shelly being pregnant flat-out poleax him?

He'd expected it, wanted it for her because she wanted so much to become a mother. Maybe he even wanted it for himself, for the satisfaction of watching and guiding a child through the stages of childhood that he'd pretty much missed with Jason.

Hell, he'd enjoyed every minute of every time he'd emptied his load deep inside Shelly's welcoming body, and he wanted to keep on enjoying her.

That was a problem, because he wouldn't be able to lie to himself anymore. He wouldn't be able to rationalize every time his cock got hard for her that it was because he wanted to uphold his part of the bargain they'd made.

He wanted Shelly. Pregnant or not. Baby or not. And if he was going to be brutally honest with himself, he'd admit he would still want her even if their marriage didn't result in him getting back liberal visitation with Jason.

That realization scared the living hell out of him. Fear didn't, however, do much to deflate the hard-on that had begun back in Dallas and blossomed the minute he got home.

Neither did a cold shower or his reminder to himself that his probably pregnant wife needed all the rest she could get after three days of riding herd on Jason and his cast.

He wouldn't wake her. As quietly as he could, Kurt slipped under the covers and closed his eyes.

But somehow she sensed his presence, because she rolled into his arms, warm and welcoming. His Shelly. Sweet, sexy Shelly.

How in hell had he spent two years seeing her almost every day, joking with her and becoming buddies, without recognizing the sexual tension? Tension that, once unleashed, had sizzled out of control.

Chapter Ten

Kurt smelled of sandalwood soap and tasted faintly of beer when she delved into his mouth with her tongue. God, she'd missed him.

But now he was here, his hard, hot flesh searing her belly while he stroked the length of her body, traced every sensitized inch of her as though relearning her by touch. Her fatigue melted away, replaced by sexual tension. Need.

"You're having my baby." He spoke so softly she barely made out the words.

"Yes."

He laid a hand on her middle, as though seeking proof his child grew there. "Are you happy?"

"It's what I wanted. The present I wanted from you, more than anything."

Anything except what she knew she couldn't have. The kind of head-over-heels, hearts and flowers romantic love Kurt made clear he didn't feel for her, didn't want for himself.

"Thank you," she said softly.

"My pleasure, Shel. A pleasure I fully intend to keep on enjoying. Often."

He bent his dark head to her breast and suckled gently while he used his hands to wake her passion, drive away all but the need to have him inside her easing the tension that flowed through every cell of her body.

His cock pulsed insistently against her thigh. But his hands and coaxing fingers moved slowly, arousing her with maddening deliberation. Drove her half wild to have him hard and fast and now when he circled her clit with the pad of one finger. She gasped at the sensation that started there and spidered out until she tingled all over.

"Easy, sweetheart."

"Please. I need you inside me. Now." She reached between them, circled his erection with both hands. "You want me, too."

"God, yes."

For just a moment he moaned as she applied gentle friction to his swollen flesh. Then he stayed her hands.

And moved between her legs.

"I can't wait."

She didn't want him to wait. She wanted him inside her, all the way.

"Fuck me. Now," she said, wrapping her legs around his hips and drawing him to her.

As though she were precious and fragile, he entered her slowly, deliciously, carefully. And though he didn't say the words she secretly longed to hear, he told her with every deliberate thrust, each taste of the sensitized skin along her neck and shoulders that he cared.

And after they came in unison, Kurt gathered her in his arms and held her as if he'd never let her go.

Was what he felt for her more than liking? More than friendship? More even than the explosive chemistry they shared? Shelly thought so when she laid her head on his chest and let the steady beat of his heart lull her to sleep.

But when morning came again, so did her doubts.

* * * * *

As Kurt dressed, he kicked himself for disturbing Shelly's rest last night.

Only an idiot could have missed the deep circles under her eyes, and he had a good idea his son was the reason for her exhaustion. He'd put a stop to Jason's shenanigans now, he decided, picking up the phone and dialing the OR.

"This is Silverman. Have the anesthesiologist hold up on knocking out my patient. I'll be starting late this morning," he told the OR supervisor. The woman didn't sound especially thrilled to have the day's cases start out behind schedule, but that was too damn bad.

As he strode to his son's bedroom, Kurt made a mental note to verbally ream the office manager who'd scheduled him to perform what promised to be an incredibly complicated limb salvage surgery so early on his first day back from Dallas.

Jason was sound asleep, his cast propped up on a pillow. It didn't look as though he'd moved since Kurt checked on him last night.

"Wake up."

Jason's eyelids fluttered, then drooped and shut again. "Go 'way."

Kurt wanted to shake his son until his teeth rattled, but he managed to restrain himself and tap Jason's shoulder instead.

"Whatcha want?" This time Jason's eyes opened and stayed that way, though Kurt didn't appreciate the sullen set of his son's mouth.

Ann Jacobs

"I want to tell you to lay off Shelly. From the looks of it, you ran her on a merry chase while I was gone."

"Not as merry a chase as I bet you ran her on when you got home last night, since you two just got married and all."

A blood vessel in Kurt's head started to pound. What the hell should a twelve-year-old know about sex anyhow? Obviously more than he'd thought likely.

"That's none of your business. I'm telling you, I won't have you running Shelly ragged. She needs her rest."

"Yeah. I noticed she looked kinda green yesterday when she brought me my breakfast. So how am I supposed to get what I need? You and Dr. Blackstone said I have to stay off this cast, and I haven't seen anybody else around here to wait on me."

Kurt glanced at the bedside table with its remote controls and an assortment of half-full glasses and packaged snacks. Crutches leaned against the headboard, within Jason's easy reach.

"It doesn't look as though you've been doing without a whole lot. You can decide now what you want to snack on today, and I'll bring it up before I leave for work."

"But what if I change my mind? Or need ice or something?"

"Tough. You don't ask Shelly to go running up and down stairs to get things you can do without. Surely your mother doesn't cater to you like this."

"Mom doesn't make me lie in bed twenty-four-seven except to go to the bathroom, either." Jason shrugged.

"If your mom had kept you down when you first hurt yourself, you wouldn't be recovering from surgery now. Tell me what you want to snack on or do without."

Kurt checked his watch. If he was lucky, he might get to the hospital in time to start his seven o'clock case by eight.

As though put upon, Jason rattled off a list of food and drink Kurt figured should be sufficient to feed a Little League baseball team after a hard game.

"I'll be back in a minute."

Since Shelly apparently had organized Jason's favorite snacks on the counter, it took very little time to stack food on a tray and fill a cooler with ice and canned drinks. When Kurt went back upstairs, he found Shelly in Jason's room.

"I'll be home early. We can play some chess if you'd like," Kurt told Jason when he set down the food. "There should be enough here to keep you from starving between meals. Take it easy on Shel, like I told you. Your brother or sister's giving her a bit of a hard time."

Jason's mouth dropped open. "What?"

"We're having a baby." Kurt put his arms around Shelly's slender waist and gave her a gentle squeeze when he noticed her cheeks turning bright pink.

"Gross. I guess Mom was right after all. She said the only reason you'd get married again was if you'd — "

"Stop while you're ahead, son. We're happy about the baby, and we hope you will be, too."

God, but he hated having to leave Shelly alone all day with Jason and his smart-ass attitude.

"What would you like for breakfast?" Shelly asked, obviously uncomfortable with the tension that crackled in the air.

Jason's brow wrinkled, as though he were considering something of earth-shattering importance. "A waffle would be good."

"Okay." Shelly wriggled out of Kurt's hold and headed out, apparently anxious to escape before the stress level rose again.

Waffles sounded okay to Kurt, too, until he recalled the ones Shelly made for their Sunday breakfasts and realized that for her, making waffles involved more than taking a couple out of the freezer and dropping them into the toaster.

"Remember what I told you, Jason. Have a care for somebody other than yourself for a change."

With that, Kurt walked out, checking his watch as he went downstairs. He needed to sit down and have a serious talk with Jason, but that would require more time than he had. As it was, he was going to have to placate a furious OR supervisor by the time he made it to the hospital.

* * * * *

"How's Jason getting along with Shelly?" Mark asked early that afternoon when Kurt ran into him in the surgeons' lounge.

Kurt stripped off his cap and mask, tossed both in the trash before sinking onto one of the faux leather sofas against the wall.

"Jason's doing fine. Whether Shelly will survive another week with him bedridden is another question." He rubbed at his right shoulder, but every muscle in his body ached.

"Long case?"

"A limb salvage on a sixteen-year-old. I replaced the femur with a titanium rod. A procedure I advised against, by the way. Bill Traub apparently talked the parents into trying it along with multiple chemo protocols, instead of going with the amputation."

"Osteosarcoma?"

"Stage Three."

Mark shook his head. "Sounds like a medical oncologist. I understand Traub wanting to try his poisons first, but on a Stage Three?"

"Exactly my position. But Traub got Gordon to book the case for me while we were gone. And there was no doubt at all that cancerous femur had to go, one way or another, if the girl is to have any chance at all for long-term survival. I hope Traub's chemo does its job on the residual cells." He wished he had more confidence that it would.

Mark rubbed at his bum knee. "Are you finished here for today?"

"Yeah." Kurt had office appointments booked, but at least the case he'd just finished was the only surgery on his list. "You?"

"I've got four outpatient arthroscopies, which means you're it for any traumas that come in."

"Great. I would be on call. I promised Jason we'd play chess tonight."

Mark shrugged. "Maybe you'll get lucky and everybody in San Antonio will be extra careful going home from work. We do occasionally have days like that, you know."

Not often enough. Chances were good he'd get called to patch someone back together again. And Kurt wouldn't ask Mark to switch emergency call with him so soon after he'd taken time off for his honeymoon.

"I'd better let Shelly know." The thought of her, warm and sleepy in his arms last night, lightened Kurt's black mood. "By the way, she's pregnant."

"Congratulations." Mark's grin went from ear to ear. "When's the happy event?"

"Nine months from our wedding night, more or less. She just took the early pregnancy test yesterday."

"Mid-January, then."

Kurt shrugged. "That sounds about right."

He dressed quickly while Mark rattled on about some of the changes he could expect in Shelly as her pregnancy advanced. Morning sickness, mood swings from euphoria to deep depression. Strange cravings for hard-to-find foods at ridiculous hours of the day and night.

"You'd think I'd know all this," Kurt said as he shrugged into a lab coat. "I suppose med school took up too much of my energy when I was going through this before. I don't recall Adrianna acting much different pregnant from the way she was any other time."

"You'd better make time to notice now, my friend. Shelly's good for you. Don't want to take a chance on losing her."

"I won't."

As he hurried to the office, Kurt gave Mark's comment serious thought. Thirteen years ago he'd viewed Adrianna's pregnancy with a detached sort of pleasure — and look how their relationship had ended. In court every few months, fighting over rights to the little boy they'd both wanted before he was born.

The little boy wasn't so little anymore. Kurt recalled Jason's knowing smirk at the news of Shelly's pregnancy, his crude implication that he knew more than he should about the physical aspects of marriage.

He wouldn't let another child become a battleground or stand by and let another marriage bite the dust. Between patients, he called home, checked on Shelly as well as Jason. And he prayed no emergency would keep him from going home tonight.

But God wasn't listening, because at three-fifteen Kurt got a call from a colleague in Tulsa. Rodeo star Trey Singleton, a local boy made good, had broken nearly every bone in his body yesterday in a freak fall from an ornery bronc.

They apparently had immobilized the fractures and delayed the major ortho work while general surgeons worked to remove his ruptured spleen and stop the internal bleeding. Now, according to Kurt's colleague, Trey was stable enough to move and he wanted Kurt to do the surgery.

"If it's safe to move him, do it," he told the other doctor, though the description of multiple compound open fractures of Trey's left leg made Kurt shudder. "He probably asked for me because I've treated him before."

"Right. He said you fixed his knee last summer. Thinks the world of you. Here's the timetable. He's coming via air ambulance to San Antonio International. He should be taking off any minute now. University Hospital's helicopter will pick him up there. He should arrive there about five o'clock, give or take."

So they'd put Trey in the air first, then called for permission to transfer him. Kurt's self-protective antennae went up. "Are you telling me everything, Doctor?" he asked, dreading the answer.

"He needs to go straight to surgery as soon as he gets to you. Frankly I didn't think I could save his leg if I operated on him. He believes you can, and I'm hoping he's right. I've had his records faxed to the hospital."

"What about his other injuries?" Kurt asked.

"Nothing challenging except the leg. But the fractured clavicle will need to be checked, and he'll need an open reduction of the compound fracture of his left wrist. That leg's broken in four places. Femur, tibia, and fibula, every one of the fractures is compound and comminuted. I've never seen anything worse. If anything needs your kind of skill, this one does."

The other doctor had dumped Kurt with what he didn't need, especially tonight: an all-night job that sounded more likely to fail than succeed.

"Thanks," he muttered, not trying to veil his sarcasm.

"Better you than me."

Kurt visualized sweat rolling down the other surgeon's forehead. And he felt moisture beading on his own brow as he okayed the transfer and slammed down the phone.

"I've got an emergency case coming in. Reschedule the rest of my appointments," he told the receptionist as he strode out of the office.

In a little more than an hour, Trey Singleton would arrive. Meanwhile, Kurt had X-rays and lab reports to study before taking the rodeo cowboy to surgery.

Thank God for cell phones. Kurt used his while making the trek to the hospital, to let Shelly know what was going on and beg off the chess game he'd promised Jason.

"I'm sorry, Shel. Will you be okay?"

She reassured him she and Jason would get along just fine and wished him luck with Singleton, whose physical therapy she'd handled after his knee surgery last summer. But she sounded tired, which made Kurt worry.

Once he saw the paperwork and realized just how mangled Singleton's leg really was, Kurt forced personal concerns from his mind and started to map out an operative plan.

Singleton obviously expected to wake up with that leg still part of his body, but Kurt couldn't guarantee that would be possible. After one last look at the records, he scrawled in the proposed operation on the hospital's standard consent form: "Attempt multiple open reductions/internal fixations of compound comminuted fractures of left femur, tibia, and fibula; possible left below knee amputation." At the end of the notation, he listed the simpler procedures necessary to repair Singleton's fractured left shoulder and arm.

What he'd proposed sounded coldly clinical, written down like that. He shook his head. Words couldn't express how hard he would work to see his patient end up with a functioning natural limb.

Four-fifteen. Not much time.

Kurt's stomach growled, reminding him he'd skipped breakfast and substituted a soggy burger in his office for a decent lunch. He'd better get something to eat or he wouldn't last through the long night ahead.

And he'd better let Mark know his own evening plans were history. Trey Singleton's injuries would provide plenty of challenge for both of them.

Stretching the kinks out of his shoulders and wishing Shelly were here to rub out the tension, Kurt headed for the dressing room and changed. Then he took the unsigned consent form to Lanie Moore, the three-to-eleven charge nurse in the OR.

"How long before Dr. Blackstone will finish his last case?" he asked when she looked up from her paperwork.

"Shouldn't be long. They took in the last patient about an hour ago."

"Get him on the intercom and let him know I'll need him to scrub in with me as soon as he's done."

Lanie looked surprised.

"Yeah, I know he's been in the OR all day, but it's going to take more than one skilled orthopedic surgeon to put Singleton back together."

"I can't believe Trey Singleton got thrown off a bronc."

From Lanie's tone, Kurt guessed Trey might be the object of a little hero worship. "Apparently he did. Have you heard when we can expect him to arrive?"

"The plane just landed. They're loading him into our helicopter."

She smiled, almost as if she was about to see the rodeo star in action. Then she glanced at the consent form and shook her head.

"This looks like it's going to take a while. Can I call the kitchen to send something for you and the other doctors to eat before you start?"

"I'd like that." It would save him a trip to the cafeteria downstairs.

While Lanie talked to someone in the kitchen, Kurt checked out the chalkboard on the wall behind her. Good. Sam Walters, chief of anesthesiology, and two senior orthopedic residents were penciled in for the case. So were four of Kurt's favorite surgical nurses. He'd be operating in the biggest and best equipped of the orthopedic rooms.

"Will you need anybody else?"

Kurt glanced her way. "Just Dr. Blackstone. You thought of everybody."

"I sent the blood work they faxed from Tulsa to the blood bank. Dr. Walters said to have them crossmatch six units of whole blood. Will that be enough?"

Kurt nodded. He hoped to hell they wouldn't need more than two, but he couldn't fault the anesthesiologist for being cautious.

"Is the room ready?" He couldn't imagine that it wouldn't be, unless someone was in there finishing a case.

"All set. I moved Dr. d'Angelo's four o'clock case to OR six. Good thing word about Mr. Singleton didn't reach us until after Mrs. Alton had left. She swore she was going to book all your cases in the worst rooms we have, after you put her behind schedule this morning."

Kurt pretended contrition, though he couldn't care less if he'd ticked off the OR supervisor. "I had family responsibilities to take care of. Home crises happen, even to surgeons. Do you think a box of Godiva chocolates might sweeten Mrs. Alton's mood?"

Lanie looked doubtful, but then she smiled. "I don't know about Mrs. Alton, Doctor, but they'd sure sweeten mine. Would you like me to call your wife a couple of times while you're in the OR, let her know how much longer you're likely to be?"

Kurt had never thought of asking anyone to do that, but the idea appealed. He'd worry less about Shelly if he knew someone would be checking in with her. And it would let her know he cared.

"I'd appreciate it." He wrote his home number on a paper and handed it over.

"Okay."

When a buzzer went off, Lanie glanced toward the automatic doors that were slowly opening. "That should be your supper."

A waiter Kurt had seen a few times in the doctors' dining room pushed a heavily-laden food cart through the swinging doors.

He gestured toward the surgeons' lounge. "I'll set the food up in there, Doc. If I leave it out here, the nurses will be on it like a swarm of locusts."

Roast turkey on dark, wheat bread, mashed potatoes, green beans, and carrots were anything but five-star fare, but Kurt appreciated the way they filled his empty belly. He passed on the canned peach and cottage cheese salad with its wilted lettuce leaf, but grabbed a hunk of German chocolate cake from a selection of cholesterol-laden desserts.

As he caught the last of the gooey coconut and pecan filling on his fork, Mark and Dr. Walters joined him in the lounge and filled their plates.

"Lanie told me Singleton's brother is in the waiting room. He wants to see you," Mark said.

Good. Kurt doubted Trey would be in any shape to give informed consent for surgery.

"I'll go see him now. Is the team ready?"

Walters nodded. "I told the residents to come grab a bite as soon as they re-check the packs."

On the way out, Kurt grabbed a piece of chocolate cream pie off the cart and dropped it off with Lanie. "Give me the consent form. I'll get Singleton's brother to sign it. Meanwhile enjoy the pie."

She looked relieved. Probably was. He doubted she'd relished asking Trey's brother to give permission for what Kurt might have to do to Trey's body.

Chapter Eleven

Lanie Moore had called again from the surgery desk, just to make sure "for Dr. Silverman" that Shelly was doing all right. Three times, yet. Shelly set the phone down, sipped her sweetened herbal tea, and wondered at Kurt's uncharacteristic concern.

"Shelly!"

What did Jason want now?

This was her third trip upstairs since she'd brought him dinner. She'd counted, even though knowing she'd counted gave her a guilty twinge.

"What do you need?" she asked when she opened the door and got bombarded with the ear-piercing noise of rap on MTV.

"I dropped the remote control."

She picked it up and set it on his chest. "There. Can I get you anything else?"

"No. Why does Dad say he wants me here, when all he does when I am is work?"

Shelly tried to brush a lock of dark hair off Jason's brow, but he caught her hand and shoved it away. "I don't need another mother. And I sure as hell don't need a father either. Not one who cares more for a bunch of strangers than he does for his own kid."

She bit her tongue to keep from commenting on her stepson's language. "Your dad loves—"

"Sure he does. How many nights do you spend in this house all alone because he's playing God with somebody's life?"

Jason's bitterness tore at Shelly's heart. "Your dad's work is important. You should meet some of his patients. I never met one who wasn't grateful he was there for them when they needed him."

"What about me? You, too? I can't believe you're gonna have *another* kid for him to ignore."

What could she say without knocking Jason's mother? The woman obviously had done a number on the boy, poisoning his mind against Kurt.

"Got nothing to say? You know I'm right, don't you?"

"No, Jason. You're not right. It's been hard for you, I'm sure, with your father living so far away. But he doesn't ignore you. Not a day goes by that he doesn't think about you. I know."

"Sure he does. He cares so much that he'd rather patch up some rodeo cowboy than spend time with me."

Kurt was right when he said Adrianna had made Jason believe he had to compete with Kurt's patients for attention. It infuriated Shelly, though her heart went out to the boy.

"That's not fair," she said, hoping somehow to get through to him. "Your dad felt terrible, breaking a promise he'd made you. But this patient's surgery couldn't wait."

The stubborn set of Jason's jaw reminded Shelly of his father. "He didn't even call me when I broke my toes."

"He didn't know about that until an hour before you got here," she said as gently as she could, considering how much she wished she could get her hands around

Adrianna's long, slender neck and squeeze her until she begged for mercy.

"I don't believe you. Mom said she called Dad."

"But she didn't."

"Whatever." Jason changed channels, then glued his gaze to the TV screen.

There had to be a way to reach him. Shelly sat on the edge of the bed and spoke softly.

"Your dad was sorry he had to bag on your chess game. Truly."

"And he'll be just as sorry next time, when the next emergency comes up."

Shelly didn't miss the boy's obvious determination not to look her way.

His gaze still on the TV, Jason continued. "I don't know why he keeps fighting Mom to have me visit more often, since he hardly takes time to say hello when I'm here."

"That's not fair."

"Fair? Was it fair for him to leave me with you while he spent the weekend out of town?"

"Your dad had agreed to speak at the conference in Dallas months ago. Long before your mom called and said you'd be coming for an unscheduled visit."

Jason shot a doubtful look at Shelly, but at least he didn't come up with another rebuttal.

That was good, because Shelly's head was swimming. She needed to lie down. "Goodnight, Jason. I'm tired, even if you're not. Don't forget to turn off the TV before you go to sleep."

"Coward," she heard him say as she closed his door.

Was she? She'd probably care in the morning, but now she was too tired to do more verbal sparring with Kurt's unhappy son.

* * * * *

Quarter to one. More than seven hours since they'd rolled Trey Singleton into OR four. The circulating nurse mopped sweat off Kurt's brow as he placed the last of three drains in the long incision on Singleton's left thigh.

"How's he doing, Sam?"

The anesthesiologist looked up from the monitor screens that were his responsibility. "Holding up remarkably well."

Walters sounded as wiped out as Kurt felt.

He took a deep breath, checked the incision one last time.

"Okay. You can close now," he told the resident who had helped him piece together shattered bone and suture torn muscles and ligaments around the femur while Mark finished piecing together smoothed down bone ends of Singleton's tibia.

The resident started stitching, then glanced at Kurt. "Are we going to put this leg in a cast?"

"Not until the antibiotics get the infection under control. We'll immobilize the leg with traction."

Mark stepped back from the table, giving the resident who'd assisted him the chance to close the other operative wound on the patient's calf. "Singleton's going to be one unhappy camper, with one end in traction and the other end in fiberglass," he said.

"Dumb cowboy better be grateful he still has this leg," Kurt snapped. "If he had a brain, he'd stay the hell away from wild horses."

Then Kurt realized how callous he sounded.

"Excuse me. That was uncalled for. It's been a long night," he said as he stepped away from the table and left the room.

By the time he talked with Trey's brother, got the ortho tech to rig a traction device, and wrote orders for the ICU nurses, it was nearly three in the morning. Too late to call Shelly.

Too late to make it worth his while to drive home. But he was going to do it anyhow.

Funny. Before he and Shelly married, he hadn't minded catching a snooze on one of the cots in the surgeons' lounge instead of walking to his bachelor apartment. Now, though, the idea of not waking and finding Shelly next to him made the trip home worthwhile.

Besides, Kurt needed to carve some time out of his schedule to spend with Jason. And he had to do it in the next few days, before his son went back to Adrianna.

* * * * *

Kurt had tried to make time. But trying hadn't gotten the job done. The last three days of Jason's visit had consisted of one patient crisis after the other. One night he hadn't made it home at all.

Shelly had understood, which was good. But Jason hadn't. The morning he left, he was understandably upset when Kurt had called to say goodbye from Trey Singleton's bedside in the ICU.

Upset enough to refuse to come to San Antonio for the Fourth of July holiday even though Kurt had arranged to be off work. Kurt clenched and unclenched the fist that wasn't holding the receiver to his ear while he listened to his attorney.

"I did everything but get down on my knees and beg Jason to forgive me. And damn it, I didn't do anything wrong except do my job," Kurt told Calvin when the lawyer suggested they postpone the custody hearing.

"It's not me you have to persuade. I feel for you. But the judge is certainly going to consider the boy's wishes, and it's obvious to me what those wishes are going to be. I'm not saying you should drop the petition, only that you need to mend some fences before we go into a hearing."

Kurt couldn't argue the point Calvin just made. But he wasn't sure time was going to heal the rift, or that Jason would listen to anything he said.

Mending fences wasn't easy when those fences had been erected by a resentful almost-teenager whose mother apparently took pleasure in upholding his semi-righteous anger. Kurt told Calvin goodbye, set down the phone, and shrugged off his lab coat.

He might not be able to placate his son, but he could show Shelly he wasn't the bastard Adrianna made him out to be. If he hurried, he could join her at her OB's office and get a look at the sonogram she'd mentioned that she'd be having this afternoon.

Her smile when he strode into the examining room made the effort worthwhile, but Kurt wished she didn't look so surprised to see him there. The baby's heartbeat, amplified as it was by the Doppler instrument, surrounded them in the small room.

"You're just in time," Brian Levy told Kurt when he moved to Shelly's side and took her hand. "Ready to see your baby?"

"Yes." Shelly squeezed Kurt's fingers.

The obstetrician turned on the portable ultrasound unit and moved the wand slowly over Shelly's rapidly expanding belly. Kurt watched the blurred images on the screen, tried to make out body parts.

"Guess I'll have to apologize for yelling at you, Shelly," Brian said, his gaze fixed not on her but on the screen. "You're not gaining weight too fast. You've got two babies in there."

"Twins?" She raised her head and squinted at the blurry image on the screen where Brian was pointing out the indistinct forms of not one but two babies.

Kurt tried hard to squelch the panic that rose when a long list of complications attendant on multiple-birth pregnancies came to mind. Funny that he'd remember now, years after having had to memorize that list for a final exam in OB-GYN. Shelly sounded shocked enough at the news, without having him come across as anything but thrilled.

"Boys or girls, Brian?" he asked, his tone a hell of a lot more cheerful than he felt.

"They're fraternal." Brian moved the wand around, zeroed in on one of the wiggling fetuses. "This one's a boy. I think the other's a girl. How about that?"

The OB's tone was hearty. Too hearty. Kurt held Shelly's hand and kept a smile pasted on his face, but when that list flooded his memory he started sweating.

Dampness beaded on his brow, and there wasn't a damn thing he could do about it.

First time mother. Over thirty. Twins. Any of the three could mean trouble. All three together spelled high-risk, in spades. The rumbling Scots burr of a long-ago OB professor resounded in his ears.

"So what do you think, Daddy?" Brian prompted.

"That's great," Kurt managed to say when the OB shot him a questioning look. But he'd damn well have a long private talk with his colleague later, when Shelly wasn't there to hear.

* * * * *

Kurt was aghast that they were having twins. He'd taken the news well on the surface, but Shelly sensed that he was pretending.

Why not? He'd gotten more than he bargained for. Not just one but two babies, and no certainty Jason would relent and give them another chance.

No assurance now that the court would even grant Kurt increased visitation, because Brian had no more than glanced at that ultrasound before he labeled her pregnancy high-risk, scheduled an amniocentesis, and ordered her to take it easy.

She pulled in the driveway, opened the garage door, and stopped her car next to Kurt's beloved Alfa.

Poor Kurt. He'd gotten a lot more than he signed on for when he married her. And his leisure time, limited enough before, had become nonexistent. He hadn't taken his classic sports car out for a ride since before Jason's unscheduled visit.

Shelly gathered her purse and the sack of groceries she'd stopped for after leaving Brian's office. Then she stared at the Alfa again. Pretty soon she wouldn't fit into it, at the rate she was going.

Not that Kurt would want to take her anywhere. He hadn't been able to get away fast enough after she finished her checkup and he walked her to her car. The kiss he brushed across her cheek had been so quick she wouldn't have noticed it if she'd blinked.

Shelly shook her head. She wasn't being fair. He might have had patients to see. Surgeries to perform. Or he might have simply needed time alone to digest how much this pregnancy was going to change their lives for the next six months.

For years. Twice the diapers, twice the feedings, twice the trips to the pediatrician. Maybe more than double the work if the babies had problems the way some multiple birth children did.

Shelly envisioned a long, tense summer at best—at worst, a disastrous end to the arrangement that was their marriage.

But life went on. As the summer days grew hotter and shorter, she and Kurt struck a balance between hope and fear, recrimination and resolve. Neither of them risked tipping that fragile balance.

When Kurt came home and told her Jason had agreed to visit them over Labor Day, Shelly fought down the fatigue that grew worse with every passing day and every added pound and concentrated on doing all she could to make the holiday one to remember.

* * * * *

As he waited at the airport with Shelly the Friday before Labor Day, Kurt wasn't at all sure Jason would be getting off the plane, even though he'd asked Mark to handle any emergencies short of newsworthy catastrophes so he could spend quality time with his son.

When they'd talked on the phone yesterday, Jason had sounded as though he'd do his best to find an excuse not to come.

Kurt craned his head to see beyond the security guards screening departing passengers. When people started streaming down the aisle from the gate he tightened his grip on Shelly's hand.

"He'll be here."

Even though Brian had assured him yesterday that Shelly and the babies were doing well, Kurt couldn't shake the nagging worry that something would go wrong. She sounded tired now, even though he'd made sure they took their time walking through the airport.

He should have made her stay home. The babies had to be taking a toll on her energy, now that she was well into her fifth month.

But Kurt had no more been able to get Shelly to wait at home than he'd succeeded in making her take it easy around the house in the days before Jason's arrival. Short of roping her and tying her to the bed, nothing he'd thought of doing could have kept her from cooking and shopping for Jason's favorite treats.

"Look, Kurt, there he is."

Strolling down the corridor from the arrivals area as though he was in no hurry whatever, Jason looked as though he might have grown another inch or two without putting on a pound. The disgruntled expression on the boy's face broadcast to Kurt the fact that his son hadn't forgiven him.

"I've got my work cut out, don't I?"

Shelly squeezed his hand. "Jason will come around. He loves you."

Kurt wasn't sure about that, but he wasn't about to let his son intimidate him. Keeping Shelly at his side, he closed the distance between them.

"Hey, Jason."

"Dad." The word came out almost like a growl, but Jason's expression lightened when he turned to Shelly. "Shelly. You've gotten a lot bigger."

She laughed. "So have you. We're glad you could come."

"Kids don't have a whole lot of choice."

Kurt bit back the retort that came to mind. "Well, we're going to have a good time this weekend. Come on, son, let's get your luggage."

Jason held up an overstuffed duffel bag. "This is it." Then he turned to Shelly. "Mom said you might as well take me shopping for school clothes while I'm here."

Kurt swallowed the oath that wanted to slip off his tongue. He should have expected something like this from Adrianna. Apparently she hadn't scheduled time away from her endless rounds of tennis, bridge, and charity events to buy Jason new clothes.

Now he'd have to spend one of the four measly days the judge had allowed him, dragging his son through clothing stores at the Riverwalk Mall.

Worse, Shelly would insist on joining them. And the last thing she needed was to spend the better part of a day on her feet.

"What say we shop on Sunday?" Shelly suggested as they made their way to the parking lot. "We've planned a surprise for you tomorrow."

* * * * *

"Is Shelly okay?" Jason asked the next morning after Kurt dragged him out of bed and coerced him into joining him while he made hospital rounds.

Kurt looked up from the chart he was reviewing in the doctor's lounge outside the surgical ICU. "She's fine. Just tired. But we need to take it easy on her. It takes a lot of energy, carrying two babies around."

"So when are they due?"

At least Jason seemed mildly interested in Shelly and his potential siblings. That was something. "Mid-January."

"Are they boys or girls?"

"One of each. You'll be getting a brother and a sister all at the same time."

Jason shrugged. "I feel sorry for them."

"Why?"

"Because the only time they'll get with you is later, when they're big enough for you to drag along while you take care of your patients."

Kurt snapped the chart shut, met his son's sullen gaze. "Is that what you think I'm doing now? Dragging you along?"

"Aren't you?"

"I guess I am, but it's not as though I get to see you every day. Come on. I'm finished here. We're going to pick up Shelly and head out to see Trey Singleton. He's invited us to go horseback riding at his family's ranch."

"Isn't he the rodeo cowboy you patched together the last time I was here?"

"He is. You've got a good memory." No wonder, Kurt thought, recalling how Trey's surgery and rocky recuperation had made him let Jason down not once but several times.

Kurt handed the chart back to a nurse at the ICU command post. "Call Mark Blackstone if my patients give you any problems this weekend. I'm signed out to him. By the way, Margie, this is my son Jason."

"I could tell. You two look too much alike not to be related." She smiled at Jason. "You like making rounds with your dad?"

"It's okay."

Jason sounded singularly unenthusiastic, but when Kurt thought about it, he realized that when he was his son's age, he hadn't been all that different. "I didn't care much for tagging along with my dad, either, when I was a kid," he commented while they waited for an elevator.

Kurt wondered if his father had felt frustrated, too. He should have exhibited a little interest in those construction projects his dad had shown him on school holidays long ago.

"If you didn't like getting dragged along with your dad, why do you make me go with you now?" Jason asked as he slid onto the passenger seat.

Kurt fit the key in the ignition. "My work's a big part of who I am. I suppose I want you to realize that what I do is important. That it's more than a good way of putting food in our mouths."

He imagined that was what his dad had wanted, too, and for the first time he understood the disappointment his family had felt when he turned his back on the business his grandfather founded and decided to become a doctor.

The Alfa roared to life, drowning out something Jason said. When Jason smiled, though, Kurt began to hope he was making progress toward restoring a loving relationship with his son.

* * * * *

Jason had to admit his dad was trying. And that their visit to Trey Singleton's ranch had been fun.

Trey Singleton must have really needed help when they'd brought him to the hospital, because he still looked like he'd been run over by a truck today.

The rodeo cowboy had laughed a lot, even when Shelly moved his arms and the leg that wasn't in a plaster cast around in ways that had to have hurt like crazy.

After a few minutes Trey had shooed Dad and Jason out to the barn so Shelly could finish his therapy, and they'd taken a ride with a Circle S ranch hand who'd gone along to show them the sights.

They'd stopped on a shady hilltop where they could see for miles. Cattle and mesquite shrubs dotted the vast expanse of land, and the occasional cowboy rode by on a horse or in a jeep. Every now and then a tumbleweed rolled lazily across the field.

The view had sent Jason's imagination soaring.

The rolling Texas hill country was nothing like the lush green hillsides outside Atlanta where he rode horseback once in a while with Mom. This was bigger. More rugged. Jason imagined covered wagons rumbling over fields that seemed to stretch out forever, clouds of dust in their wake.

Dad sat his horse like a pro. That hadn't surprised Jason, because his father wasn't the kind of guy to do anything halfway.

What had surprised him was that Dad seemed to enjoy the ride. According to Mom, all Dad had ever liked to do was work.

And what Jason had seen on his last trip here supported her claim that Dad didn't care about people unless they were broken in a million pieces, the way Trey had been.

But as they drove back toward San Antonio, Jason wasn't sure anymore.

"Are you okay?" Dad reached over and squeezed Shelly's hand.

She nodded and murmured something Jason couldn't make out. It didn't seem to him that Shelly doubted Dad's concern or that Dad made her unhappy.

Whatever. Shelly was a great cook. Jason dug into the basket stowed behind his seat and fished out another brownie.

"Want one?" he asked when he noticed Dad glance at him through the rearview mirror.

"Yeah. You can't resist Shelly's brownies either, can you?"

"They're pretty good." Jason wasn't ready to admit to more than that. It wasn't fair to Mom, even if she didn't cook at all.

But he was beginning to get another picture of Dad. What he did for his patients *was* valuable. What Dad had done for Trey Singleton had even been important enough, maybe, that Jason ought to excuse him for breaking his promise that night when he saved Trey's leg.

Jason didn't believe the only people Dad ever thought about were his patients, and he was beginning to doubt Mom's theory that Dad wanted more time with him only to spite her.

Maybe Dad hadn't cared enough for Mom, but it seemed obvious that he liked Shelly a lot.

Dad must love him, too. It didn't make sense that he'd go to so much trouble to keep in contact with somebody he didn't care about. Or that he'd start a custody fight just to spite Mom. Not when Mom insisted Dad hadn't cared how she felt about anything even when they were married.

Yeah.

Jason wasn't ready to let Dad off the hook quite yet, but he guessed he could cut him some slack. After all, Jason wasn't a baby. He could make up his own mind who he wanted to spend his time with.

He didn't have to believe everything Mom said. And he didn't have to hate Dad or feel disloyal to Mom.

Besides, he had fun with his dad, and Shelly was cool even if she wasn't drop-dead gorgeous like his mom.

By the time they finished their Labor Day picnic the following Monday and Dad took him to catch a plane home, Jason was sort of looking forward to his next visit.

* * * * *

The following week Shelly met Kurt in Calvin's office. The babies tumbled and kicked, as though they sensed their mother's worry.

"I've got good news and bad news," the lawyer said when Kurt asked why they'd been summoned.

Shelly choked down the nausea that attacked her when Kurt's expression tightened.

"Let's hear it."

Calvin grinned. "You two must have done something right last weekend. Jason told the judge he wants to spend more time here with you."

Kurt let out his breath and squeezed Shelly's hand. "Great. What's the kicker?"

"The judge won't make any change in visitation until your babies are born. Adrianna's lawyer argued successfully that Shelly's in no condition to ride herd on Jason now, while she's carrying twins."

"No!" Shelly could hardly believe her ears. Kurt wouldn't have his son, and it was all her fault.

"It's all right, honey. At least Jason's not fighting against coming here now."

Calvin cleared his throat. "I tried, but it wasn't possible to argue away the fact that the pregnancy's considered high-risk."

"So what do we do now?"

"Wait. You'll get Jason for a week over the Christmas holidays. That's in the current visitation agreement. Kurt, you'll have to take off from work again."

"No problem," Kurt said.

But it would be a problem. Shelly could see it in his hooded gaze. He knew as well as she that Mark would want time off during the holidays, too — time to spend with his own family. December was one of the ripest times of year for trauma, and Kurt would have to take his share of the emergencies even if Jason was with them.

How long would they have to live on the edge, not knowing how a judge in Atlanta would rule?

Calvin apparently didn't feel the tension in the room. "Okay," he said, closing the folder on his desk.

"Then what, after the babies are born?" Shelly asked.

"Then, assuming Jason still feels the same, we'll take our case to the judge again."

So nothing was decided. Nothing would be, until after she had the babies she'd begged Kurt to give her. Guilt washed over her, though she tried to smile at Kurt as they left Calvin's office.

Chapter Twelve

By the time Thanksgiving loomed around the corner, Shelly had to agree the Atlanta judge had a point when she'd intimated that a woman pregnant with twins was no match for an active twelve-year-old.

As she'd gotten heavier and more awkward, she sensed Kurt pulling away from her, not just physically but emotionally. He'd never done that before.

Though he still held her at night, he buried himself in his work more than ever. And when he was with her, he was uncharacteristically quiet. Shelly missed her best friend.

And she had no idea how to get him back.

Sometimes she wondered how she'd get through the next eight weeks. Her back ached all the time, and her feet swelled like water balloons every time she forgot to sit often and prop them up. The simplest activities had become daunting chores.

She had to get off it, walk out on her self-pity party. Maybe she'd make those apples Donna had brought over last weekend into a pie for Kurt. Or applesauce.

Just then the twins staged a kickboxing exhibition in her belly, and Lynn Blackstone appeared at the kitchen door.

Glad for the distraction, Shelly waddled to greet her friend.

"So how are the little ones treating you?" Lynn asked as she set down her tote bag and took a seat at the kitchen table.

"They're beating me up at the moment. Coffee?"

Lynn smiled. "If it's handy."

Shelly poured coffee for Lynn and a glass of milk for herself. "How's work?"

"Killer. I started therapy on one of Kurt's patients yesterday. You'd better be grateful, my friend, because I'm taking the brunt of his awful moods—what he isn't inflicting on the office staff and surgical teams, that is."

"Kurt's not irritable." At least he had never been, with her. "He's concerned about his patients."

Lynn shook her head. "He's not ornery to you. Never was, even before you two got married. Believe me, though, when I say surly is too mild a word to describe the way he's acting at work. I'd almost think he was the one pregnant with twins."

"It's the custody petition. The judge won't make a decision until after our babies are born. The waiting has Kurt a little crazy."

"He's a lot crazy, if you ask me." Lynn frowned. "Kurt's not blaming you, is he?"

"No. He hasn't said a mean word to me about anything." Kurt had hardly said a word to her, period, and he got quieter and moodier every day. "But I know it's tearing him apart not to see Jason. If I hadn't wanted a baby so much—"

"Wait a minute here. Are you telling me you got pregnant all by yourself?"

"Of course not. But I'm the one who wanted a baby. Kurt kept his promise, but I haven't."

Lynn looked Shelly in the eye. "What are you talking about?"

"Kurt married me because he wanted his visitation with Jason restored. His lawyer said he needed to show the judge a suitable home and stable care arrangements for that to happen. I've let him down—"

"Wait a minute. The way I see it, you've done wonders with this place."

"But I'm in no condition now to ride herd on Jason, or so says the judge. The way I'm feeling now, I've got to agree."

Lynn murmured her sympathy, then glanced at her watch. "I've got to run. You take care and think happy thoughts about your babies. Remember they'll be here in less than two months."

"I'll try."

"For God's sake, quit beating yourself up over things you can't help."

After Lynn left, the babies started kicking again, as though they'd been listening and didn't like taking the blame for Mommy or Daddy's uneasy emotional state. As if her touch might soothe them, Shelly laid a hand over her tummy and hummed an off-key rendition of a lullaby while she summoned the energy to peel apples.

* * * * *

His office appointments finished for the day, Kurt drummed on his desk with his fingers. He should go through some old case records for the paper he needed to write, but couldn't dredge up the necessary enthusiasm.

He missed Jason, and he found it harder every day to hold on to his temper. If only Adrianna hadn't decided to use the boy as a weapon, he'd have his son more than a couple of weeks a year.

Dead leaves from the oak tree outside his window swirled in the strong breeze. In a couple of days they'd be celebrating Thanksgiving. Damn it, Jason should be spending the holiday with him.

Tonight Jason would be winding up his soccer season. The last before he'd move up to a tougher league. Kurt had spoken to him on the phone, but that was a poor substitute for being there in person.

Another milestone he'd be missing out on. Another part of his son's childhood Kurt wouldn't get to experience.

It was hell, having to wait until mid-January to settle Jason's future. And Kurt had gone a couple of knockdown rounds with Mark this morning over his need to take a week off during the height of the Christmas rush.

Damn it, Mark had his kids all the time. As of now, all Kurt had to look forward to with Jason was a lousy week of his son's winter holidays.

But that wasn't Mark's fault. Kurt slid his chair away from the desk and got up, intending to find his partner and apologize.

When he looked up, Mark was standing in the doorway.

"Thought I'd stop by and see how Bobby Duran is doing." Mark must have seen their mutual patient's name on the appointment book for this afternoon.

Kurt grinned, reached in his pocket, pulled out a five-dollar bill, and sent it sailing in his partner's direction.

Mark grabbed the five, pocketed it. "What's this for?"

"Our bet. Remember?"

"Oh. Yeah."

"You were right. The leg was salvageable after all. Bobby's not likely to be running marathons, but eventually he ought to be able to walk with no more than a limp."

Kurt picked up Bobby's chart, handed it to his partner. "Here. Read for yourself. Duran's recovery's the only good news I've heard today."

"Trouble?"

"Times three. Two patients, one ex-wife."

Mark raised an eyebrow. "Want to elaborate?"

"One, I had to admit Trey Singleton to the hospital this morning. He's going to need more surgery. Two, Traub's chemo didn't do the job for the patient I did the limb salvage on after the conference in Dallas. She died last night. Three, having to fight with Adrianna over Jason is getting to me. But I apologize for my fit of temper. I shouldn't have taken my frustration out on you."

"Think nothing of it. By the way, we'll work out that holiday on-call schedule somehow so you can have your time with Jason. I can't imagine not seeing my kids every day."

Kurt shrugged. "You're not married to Adrianna."

"Neither are you, now."

"A fact for which I'm incredibly grateful."

Thank God he had Shelly now, because without her calm support, Kurt imagined he'd be ready for a straitjacket. Though he had plenty of patients to keep him busy and those patients had more than enough problems to challenge him, the uncertainty about Jason never strayed far from his mind.

Mark took a seat, then met Kurt's gaze. "Lynn said she stopped by to see Shelly this morning," he said. "She's worried about her."

"Why?" Did Lynn know something about Shelly and the babies that Kurt didn't?

"She says Shelly blames herself because of the holdup on the custody decision. Apparently she believes she's let you down."

"That's insane."

Mark shrugged. "Sometimes women's logic doesn't work the way ours does. Lynn didn't think Shelly looked well."

"Carrying twins can't be the easiest thing in the world on a woman. Shelly's just uncomfortable, and frustrated because she can't do everything she wants to do."

Or was it worry and misplaced guilt that had put those dark circles under Shelly's eyes?

Self-loathing stabbed Kurt in the gut. He'd shown Shelly little enough consideration as the pregnancy progressed, and even less joyful anticipation of the babies who were sapping her strength. Babies that were as much his as hers, but whom he'd practically forgotten in the heat of his fight to wrestle more time with Jason from Adrianna.

Mark shook his head. "I don't get it. If Lynn were the one seven months along with twins, I'd be a basket case."

"And I'm not?"

"Well, if you are, my friend, you've got a strange way of showing it. If anything, you've increased your patient load. You're here from dawn to dark and sometimes long after that. You're micro-managing your patients' rehab—"

"Obviously Lynn mentioned the disagreement we had yesterday. She took it personally."

"Kurt—"

"Do you think I just might be micro-managing, as you call it, because I'm used to booking my post-op patients with Shelly and she's not available? Lynn and I have never seen eye to eye on how far to push my patients."

"That excuse might fly if Lynn were the only one complaining that you're as ill-tempered as a wounded bear. But she isn't." Mark stood. "Why don't you take off and spend the evening with your wife for a change? I'll take call for you."

Kurt made himself smile as he stood and grabbed his jacket. After all, it wasn't all that often that his partner volunteered to take an extra night on call.

"Sounds good. I'm out of here, before you come to your senses and rescind your offer."

"Pay attention to your wife. She needs you."

Mark's words rang in Kurt's ears as he drove home through rush hour traffic, but at least Jason and the stalled custody petition didn't monopolize his thoughts.

* * * * *

A surprised smile lit Shelly's flushed face when Kurt walked through the kitchen door and inhaled something that smelled awfully good. He pulled her into his arms.

"You're home early," she said when he broke a long, arousing kiss and shed his jacket.

"Mark volunteered to take call for me. I wasn't about to turn him down." He sniffed the air again, couldn't quite identify the delicious aroma. "What's cooking?"

"Applesauce. Those apples Donna brought me the other day weren't going to last if I tried to store them raw. I thought I'd make myself some potato pancakes to go with the applesauce, but I can fix something more substantial since you're home."

"Not necessary, Shel. If you want, we can go down to the Mercado or somewhere on the Riverwalk and have dinner. If not, potato pancakes and applesauce will suit me fine."

Kurt didn't like the pallor beneath Shelly's flushed cheeks, or the circles under her eyes that seemed to have grown deeper and darker since this morning.

She looked at him, as though to figure out what he'd rather do. Then she sighed. "I'm a little tired. Let's stay home if you don't mind."

When Shelly turned back to the bubbling stuff on the stove and rubbed her lower back as though it pained her, Kurt stepped in and took over.

He spied a box of potato pancake mix on the counter and figured he could handle throwing it together. "Want to go lie down and let me make the pancakes?"

"I'm not so tired that I'd risk you cooking. But what you're doing to my back feels awfully good. You don't have to stop."

Apparently somewhere along the line Kurt had given Shelly the impression that despite having gotten through eight years of college and medical school, he was incapable of reading and following directions well enough to produce an edible meal.

"Hey, Shel, you hurt my feelings. Don't you think I can make pancakes from a mix?"

She laughed. "I'm sure you can, but you shouldn't have to. You've worked hard all day."

"And you haven't?" Hauling around the weight of two babies had to be exhausting, not to mention that she took care of most of the housework as well as shopping and fixing all their meals.

How many times should Kurt have been rubbing Shelly's back instead of letting her work the kinks out of his neck and shoulders after long days in surgery? He should have realized before that she needed a lot more help now.

One of the accusations Adrianna had made when she threw him out rang in his ears. She'd called him a selfish son of a bitch, and he supposed he had been.

It seemed he still was.

Guilt gripped him, because night after night he'd leaned into Shelly's willing hands, taken the comfort she offered even though she was the one who needed tender loving care. A lot more care than he'd been giving her.

"You're tense tonight," she said, leaning the back of her head against his chest.

That was typically Shelly, sensing his mood. Thinking of his needs and ignoring her own.

Kurt stroked her back again, then laid his hands on her shoulders. "I'm sorry, Shel. I imagine I'll be pretty much this way until we get Jason's custody situation straightened out."

If he hadn't been so stressed himself, he probably wouldn't have noticed the almost imperceptible tightening of her muscles beneath his fingers.

The uncertainty about Jason apparently was taking its toll on her, too, at a time when she shouldn't be worrying about anything.

Damn it to hell. He shouldn't have let anything tarnish her joy in planning for the arrival of their twins.

She turned to face him, her expression full of regret. "I'm so sorry, Kurt. I know the delay is my fault."

"What?"

She didn't really believe that. Or did she?

"Come over here and sit. We need to talk."

He slid a chair back from the table and waited for her to settle in before sitting beside her and taking her hand.

Her eyes looked suspiciously bright when she met his gaze. "Don't pretend you don't know, or that it doesn't run through your mind every day the way it does mine.

"Here. I'll say it out loud. If I hadn't gotten pregnant right away, if I hadn't been so sick the first few months, and if Brian hadn't tagged this pregnancy high-risk, Adrianna's attorney couldn't have persuaded the judge I'm in no shape to take care of Jason."

Kurt searched his memory. He couldn't recall ever having said or done anything to make Shelly think he blamed her for the stalemate the custody battle had reached. But somehow he must have made her believe he did.

"You're way off-base. Without you that judge would have turned my petition down flat."

Needing to reassure her further, he reached over and patted her distended belly. "Besides, if I remember correctly, I had as much to do with putting these babies in here as you did. And I enjoyed every minute of it."

"But I asked you to. You held up your end of the bargain, but I dropped the ball on mine." She blinked back tears. "Damn it, I can't seem to keep from crying. Pregnant hormones, I guess."

He wiped a tear off her cheek. "More likely you're crying because you've got a beast for a husband, if you believe I blame you for a situation that's a hell of a lot more my fault than yours."

"No. You're no beast. Actually, you're a whole lot better husband than you led me to believe you'd be. I've got no complaints."

A smile lit her face and made him want to haul her into his arms.

He yearned to unleash the jumbled emotions inside him. Affection. Gratitude. And desire.

Yeah, there was plenty of that despite her advanced pregnancy.

Kurt acknowledged the concerns of friendship, too, his need to care for his best friend's feelings the way Shelly always cared for his.

But there was more. Much more. He wanted to protect her, cherish her, care for her far beyond the terms of the arrangement they'd made.

He yearned to make the kind of home with Shelly that his parents had made for him. The sort of loving home he'd left to pursue a dream that wasn't theirs.

After his initial anger had cooled, Kurt regretted the rift that decision had caused. And he would probably have tried to mend it if he hadn't married Adrianna, an Atlanta debutante who thought his working-class roots were something best buried and forgotten.

Kurt wanted to love and be loved, something he'd sworn he'd never risk again after the debacle of his first marriage.

And that scared him to death, so he took the coward's way out.

"What say I get busy making dinner while you rest your feet, then? I've got something in mind for later, something I think you'll like."

Chapter Thirteen

After they ate, Kurt didn't retire to the library the way he'd been doing most nights when he was home. Instead, he helped Shelly load the dishwasher, then suggested they try out the fireplace in their bedroom.

While she turned back the covers on the bed, she watched him coax a small fire to life in the wrought iron grate. In the semi-darkness of the room, firelight played across his face and limned his long, lean body with a surreal sort of glow.

She loved him more each day, wanted him with every fiber of her being. But loving him in secret no longer satisfied her needs. Shelly wanted to let him know the feelings she kept locked deep inside. And she wanted him to love her back.

Crackling pine bark and water bubbling in the adjacent bathroom punctuated the silence. Kurt must have turned the hot tub on when he came upstairs earlier to change.

"How about us soaking in the hot tub?" he asked once the fire got going.

"I'd love it."

How many times in the past few weeks had she longed to feel those jets pulsing away on muscles strained by carrying around the unwieldy extra weight of her pregnancy—but passed on the pleasure because she didn't want to risk falling?

Too many to count.

Not even the knowledge that those bright fluorescent lights in the bathroom would reveal every inch of her ungainly body to her husband's gaze dimmed her anticipation. So what if Kurt thought she looked like a baby elephant when he got a good look at her without her clothes?

Shelly toed off her deck shoes and wrestled her way out of the tent-like sweater she had on. But her fingers balked at unclasping the industrial-strength white cotton maternity bra that restrained breasts grown to proportions she wouldn't have believed possible until she'd seen them mushroom practically overnight.

"Need some help?"

She nodded.

When he came up behind her and splayed his hands over her swollen breasts, Kurt was already naked. Gloriously naked and semi-aroused. It had been a week or so since he'd reached for her in the dark and they'd made gentle love.

Too long. Having him touch her like this in the firelight, feeling his hot breath tickle her hair and listening to him exhale when her nipples tightened against his palms, slammed her hormone-driven libido into overdrive.

He had her bra off and her slacks and panties around her ankles with one efficient sweep of his hands. Then he scooped her, monster belly and all, into his arms, and strode toward the bathroom.

"Let's get you into the tub. I don't want you to catch a chill."

Chill? He had to be kidding. Every cell in her body burned where her skin touched his.

He paused at the open door, dimmed the light.

"Kurt, put me down. You'll break your back."

"Hardly. You have grown some more, though." He set her onto the ledge of the hot tub, then climbed into the water and helped her get down onto the seat.

"M-mmm. Feels great." Needles of hot water pulsed against her lower back while coconut-scented steam filled her nostrils.

Kurt knelt in the foaming, whirling water and cradled her swollen breasts in his hands.

"Close your eyes. Relax. Let me love you." He bent his head, drew an aching nipple into his mouth.

Waves of pure need engulfed her.

He moved one hand lower, caressed the huge mound of her belly. A baby kicked once. Twice. Again. Pressure built between her legs, and her clit hardened in anticipation.

"Please, Kurt."

He sucked her nipple one last time, then let it go and blew gently on the dampened nub. "I can hardly wait to watch you nurse our babies. "

Her nipples tingled. She imagined Kurt's eyes darkening with desire when he watched their babies nurse. As she threaded her fingers through his soft, dark hair, an incredible tenderness washed over her.

"God. I had no idea how much it would turn me on, seeing you ripe and full of life like this." He sounded as though he were in pain.

She couldn't help laughing. "Full is the operative word. I feel like an elephant."

"You look beautiful. Incredibly sexy." When he splayed both hands over her distended abdomen, he smiled.

If she hadn't fallen in love with him long ago, she'd have succumbed instantly when he mouthed that ego-bolstering lie. For a minute, she even believed he meant it. She thought she sensed love in his gorgeous slate-gray eyes and the gentle heat of his hands as they skimmed over her very pregnant body.

His beautiful, swollen cock jutted sharply upward against his belly, leaving her with no doubt about his desire.

Kurt wanted her more at that moment than he'd ever wanted a woman.

Shelly's soft hair curled around her face in the warm, moist air. Her cheeks bloomed with color that almost wiped away the dark circles around her eyes. Her sweet lips tempted him to taste them and her swollen breasts made his mouth water with anticipation.

Water swirled around them, caught him up in a world where nothing existed but the two of them. Friends and lovers, forever linked now, no matter what the future might hold.

He stroked her belly, experienced secondhand the vigorous activity of their babies. His babies, not yet born but as worthy of his love as Jason.

His wife, who deserved all the caring emotions he had left in his wounded soul.

He slid his hand deeper in the water, found her incredibly responsive little clit. As though to give him better access, she slid her legs farther apart and leaned back against the rim of the tub.

Blood slammed into his cock, made him groan. "Shel."

With one hand, she found and stroked his cock. "M-mmm. That feels good. Really good."

She had that right. It felt too damn good, because a slippery hot tub was hardly a safe place to make love with a hugely pregnant partner. He caught her hand and brought it to his lips.

"Let's get out of here and go to bed. I want to make love to you."

She smiled, stretched her arms out on top of the swirling water. "I don't think the babies and I can move."

"I'll help." He'd done far too little of that these past months, but if he had it in him to change, he was going to do it.

He got out of the hot tub first, then steadied her as she climbed awkwardly over the rim. Before she could turn to quivering gooseflesh in the chilly air, he wrapped her in a thirsty bath sheet and hauled her into his arms.

Then he set her on the edge of their bed and went down on his knees.

"What—"

"Hush. Lie back and rest your legs over my shoulders. I want to make you come this way first."

"But what about—"

"I can wait. This is for you. Relax and let me do the work tonight."

"But you...I'm too—"

"You're gorgeous. And I'll like it too. Trust me." He skimmed his hands over her distended belly, was rewarded with an energetic kick.

Her embarrassment was palpable in a silence broken only by the crackling of a log on the fire and the pounding of his own heart, but she did as he said.

Gently, he spread her outer lips with his fingertips and blew on the sensitive flesh awaiting his attention. The slick, hot proof of her arousal nearly took his sanity.

God, he wanted to lose himself in her right now. But he wanted to pleasure her more.

She gasped when he found her clit and flicked it with his tongue. But when he covered her with his mouth and applied gentle suction, she angled her hips upward, as though to urge him on.

She reminded him of a statue he'd once seen of a fertility goddess. Sweet. Erotic. And his.

Only his.

He reached up, chafed her beaded nipples with his open palms, then stroked the hard, distended mound that held their babies. His son and daughter.

"Kurt. Don't stop." Her breath sounded ragged, her words slurred.

He tongued her harder, exulted in the strength of her release. When she started to come down, he joined her on the bed, lay on his side behind her, and entered her very carefully from behind.

He fucked her gently, the penetration shallow so as not to hurt her or their babies. But it felt good. Better than good. It felt right to be inside her, cock to pussy, with nothing in between.

When he came a few minutes later, it was more than simply a sexual release. Yet Kurt still couldn't bring himself to name what he was feeling love.

Later, when sleep eluded him, he got up so he wouldn't disturb Shelly and stared into the embers from the first fire of the season. If only he could be with Jason, make up for the times he'd not been there for his son...

But he couldn't. And he had no one to blame but himself. Not even Shelly, as much as she seemed determined to shoulder responsibility for the judge's delay in making a decision.

* * * * *

Taking blame to oneself must have been contagious, Kurt decided the next morning. At the very least there seemed to be a minor epidemic of the malady. First Shelly. Now everybody he ran into was blaming himself for something.

Over coffee, Kurt listened while Bill Traub spent fifteen minutes second-guessing himself for believing conservative surgery and aggressive chemotherapy might have cured his young patient's bone cancer.

"I couldn't even buy her six lousy months, damn it."

"Don't beat yourself up. Her prognosis wouldn't have been that much better if she'd had the amputation," Kurt said, though he imagined it would be a long time before the oncologist set aside his regret about the pretty teenager who'd died the previous day.

Even Kurt's patients seemed determined this morning to blame themselves for whatever misfortune had befallen them. Almost finished with hospital rounds, Kurt grabbed Trey Singleton's chart and headed to his room.

"I've scheduled you for surgery tomorrow," he said.

"Do what you have to, Doc. I've got no one to blame for this but me," Trey said, gesturing toward his battered left leg. "Just do it good, because I expect to be back on the rodeo circuit come spring."

Kurt doubted that would happen, but then he'd never thought Bobby Duran's leg would hold him up again, either, and he'd been proven wrong.

"Gotcha, cowboy," he said as he scribbled preoperative notes in Trey's chart. "See you in the morning."

Yeah, self-flagellation was the order of the day. One thing for sure, Kurt would make certain he made Shelly believe he didn't blame her for a damn thing.

He'd get his nurse to reschedule his afternoon appointments and take her out for dinner, somewhere quiet and luxurious.

That thought gave Kurt a jolt. What had possessed him? He never before short-changed his patients to pursue his personal pleasures.

But he knew now that sometimes he should. Mark had the right idea when he considered his family first, his career second.

* * * * *

Three hours later, when Kurt was an hour into a complicated bone graft procedure, Mark came into the operating room. Out of the corner of his eye, Kurt saw him scrubbing his hands and arms, watched a circulating nurse help him into gown, mask and gloves.

What the hell was going on? Kurt hadn't called for assistance. The senior resident who was already scrubbed in on the case could probably have performed this operation by himself.

Mentally shrugging off his partner's unexpected presence as the result of another OR snafu, Kurt concentrated on the case. He rasped rough edges off the cut ends of the patient's tibia in preparation for attaching the bone ends to a titanium rod that would replace a four-inch segment of bone that had been crushed when the patient wrecked his trail bike.

Mark tapped Kurt on the shoulder. "Move over. I'll finish here."

Suddenly apprehensive, Kurt handed over the instrument, then stepped back so Mark could take his place.

"What's going on?"

"Suction, please." Mark paused while the resident cleared the operative field. "Shelly's in labor."

And in bad trouble. Mark wouldn't have taken over a case midstream if she weren't.

Kurt swallowed an anguished cry. "She's here?"

"Upstairs. Brian Levy's with her. Go on. She needs you. I'll take care of your patients."

"I'm out of here. Thanks."

For seconds Kurt might as well have been glued to the OR floor, because he couldn't move. When he finally made his feet move, he shot out of the OR and the surgical suites as if the hounds of hell were on his tail.

Chapter Fourteen

"I'm Dr. Silverman. Where's my wife?"

As he sprinted past the nurses' station, a nurse yelled at him. "Doctor. You can't go back there like that."

"Watch me."

Another nurse blocked his way.

"Move or I'll go right through you." He had to get to Shelly.

She touched his sleeve, spoke softly. "Look at yourself. You need to change."

Shit. He'd violated every rule in the book, leaving the OR in a bloody gown and gloves. "Sorry. Where?"

"In there. Let me help you out of that gown."

When Kurt had stripped and grabbed clean scrubs off a shelf, Brian Levy, Shelly's obstetrician, hurried in and started changing.

"What's going on? Where's Shelly?" Kurt asked as he tugged on clean scrub pants and fumbled with the string at the waist.

"Delivery room three. She calmed right down when the nurses told her you're here."

"Damn it, why is she here? It's too soon."

"Placental abruption. No way to predict them, you know."

Kurt didn't. Other than recalling that the condition could be fatal, he was damned if he could remember why it happened or how it was treated. Brian might as well have been talking to a layman, though he obviously didn't realize that.

"What are you going to do?"

"C-section. They're prepping her now."

"What about the babies?"

"The head of neonatology and a couple of residents are on their way. They'll take care of them as soon as I get them out."

"I want to see Shelly."

Brian bent and pulled on nonconductive shoe covers. "Go on in, but for God's sake wipe that terrified look off your face. I'll pull her through. And I've delivered babies earlier than thirty-four weeks' gestation who've ended up just fine."

Shelly looked like hell. So did her vital signs that blinked obscenely at him from the bank of monitors.

Kurt remembered Brian's warning and pasted a smile on his face before he got in her line of vision.

"I'm here now, Shel." He bent and kissed her cool, pale lips, then latched on to her hand.

"I'm glad. Kurt, I'm so sorry—"

"Hush, sweetheart, it's not your fault. Like Brian said, these things sometimes happen."

God, don't let her die.

She had to make it, because life without her would be no life at all.

"I want to stay awake, hold our babies when they're born. Please."

Kurt glanced at the anesthesiologist, who shook his head.

"No can do, Shel."

"Then you'll stay? And hug our babies for me?"

"I'm not going anywhere. Honey, you're going to sleep in a minute or so. I'll be right here when you wake up."

It wouldn't be long now. Brian had scrubbed. Another doctor took his place at the sink, and two residents came in rolling transport isolettes.

"Don't let Brian sacrifice the babies." Shelly's fingers tightened around Kurt's hand.

"He won't."

Her eyelids drooped, but she kept fighting the anesthetic. "He told me he couldn't guarantee they'd make it."

"Don't worry. You know doctors can't go around making guarantees. Our malpractice rates would soar if we did. Go to sleep, sweetheart. Trust me. Our babies will be fine." Kurt hoped he sounded more confident than he felt.

"Promise?"

"Yeah. I promise. You relax now." He wasn't God, but what else could he say?

She smiled, then closed her eyes. "I love you, Kurt," she murmured, and then her grip on his hand slackened.

That smile made having lied to her worthwhile. Her declaration made Kurt feel about two inches high, because he suddenly realized he loved her too.

She couldn't die on him. Not now. He hadn't told her yet that she'd wormed her way into his heart in spite of his determination not to let her in.

When Brian made the first incision, Kurt felt the cut as though the knife had gone into his own gut. Not since he was a medical student observing his first operation had he come so close to passing out.

"Pressure's dropping." The anesthesiologist read out the numbers, then hung a unit of whole blood. Kurt shuddered, helpless to do more than pray Brian was as good at his business as hospital gossip claimed.

Brian lifted out a tiny infant and handed it quickly to a nurse. In seconds he brought out the other baby and passed it off to the resident who'd taken the nurse's place.

Neither baby made a sound. Kurt held his breath. Damn it, they had to live. He'd given Shelly his word.

In a corner of the delivery room, the neonatologist bent over one baby, a resident over the other. One tiny whimper followed another.

Kurt exhaled. Maybe, just maybe he hadn't lied.

The circulating nurse touched Kurt's shoulder. "Congratulations, Dr. Silverman. You've got a boy and a girl. Your wife said she wanted you to hold them before we take them to the NICU."

Helpless to do anything else for Shelly now, he dragged his gaze away, then moved across the room to pass along their mother's love to the twins.

His daughter would fit in the palm of his hand. His son wasn't a whole lot bigger. Both perfectly formed, they had his dark hair, but their pale skin looked so fragile he was afraid to touch them.

So little. So helpless. So wanted by him as well as by the woman he loved.

"What are their chances?" he asked, not at all certain he was ready to hear the answer.

The chief of neonatology glanced up over his mask. "Fifty-fifty, on paper. But they've got good reflexes. And their lungs seem well-developed. Go on. Talk to them. Give them each a hug. I've always believed premature babies sense it when their parents are pulling for them."

Very gently Kurt lifted his daughter and held her against his heart.

"How's Daddy's little girl? You're mighty pretty like your mommy. Hang in there for us, Princess," he told her, and she wrapped her tiny hand around his little finger as though to reassure him she was going to try.

Then he laid her in the isolette and picked up his son. Shelly's son. "Hey there, Tiger. You take care now. I love you. Your mommy's going to adore you, too."

Kurt choked back tears. He recalled taking his first look at Jason, who'd been big and robust and safely ensconced in the newborn nursery the first time he'd seen him. These babies were so fragile, so tiny by comparison.

The resident by his daughter's isolette cleared his throat. "Dr. Silverman, we need to get the babies to the NICU now."

"All right."

When he laid his son down, Kurt's arms felt empty.

All he could do was watch Brian sweat as he struggled to cauterize bleeders, and look with horror at the monitors that showed Shelly slipping away from him before his eyes.

He'd never felt more helpless in his life.

Then she rallied. Maybe he'd get the chance to show her how much he loved her after all.

"She's going to be okay," Brian told Kurt when he'd closed the incision. "Should be good as new in a few weeks."

As he held her hand in the recovery room, Kurt mouthed a silent prayer of thanks. And when she woke and asked him about their babies, her voice was the sweetest sound he'd ever heard.

* * * * *

Still wearing wrinkled blue scrubs, he was snoring lightly in a reclining chair by her bed when she woke up. His stubble-darkened cheeks looked hollow, as though he'd gone through hell. Shelly guessed he had.

But Kurt had obviously kept his promise. He hadn't left her.

"They're going to make it, sweetheart," he'd said when she woke up in recovery and realized again that the babies had been born too soon.

Had he also told her he loved her? Or had that been wishful thinking?

A huge bouquet of yellow roses took up nearly all the space on the bedside table. Shelly smiled when she noticed two balloons suspended above the bed, one blue and the other pink.

Her breasts felt full enough to burst, and a dull ache in her belly reminded her she'd just had major surgery. An IV dripped fluids through the needle stuck in her left hand. But she was alive, and so were her babies.

She wanted to see them.

Kurt shuddered, then opened his eyes. When she smiled at him, he jerked the recliner back upright and stood. "Are you okay?"

"I want to see our babies."

Holding her gaze, he bent and kissed her.

"I'll take you upstairs as soon as Brian comes in and checks you."

"You saw them?"

He smiled. "Yeah. I even got to hold them for a minute before they got whisked away to the NICU. Shel, they're beautiful. Thank you."

"Thank *you*."

He'd given her what she'd asked for. Twice over. Shelly bit her tongue to keep from asking him if he'd really given her what she wanted most of all—his love.

"Did you let Lynn and Mark know?" she asked instead.

"Mark stopped by recovery after he finished up my case yesterday. I'm sure he told Lynn. I also called Donna. She said to tell you she'd come see you sometime today."

"What about Jason?"

"He sends his love. I told him to call this afternoon so he could talk to you."

"You should call your parents," Shelly said.

"I already did."

"I'd love for them to come see their new grandchildren." Shelly sensed Kurt would like to ease whatever differences had caused the estrangement from his family, but she didn't want to push.

"Maybe next summer I'll take you to meet them and prove I didn't hatch in a lab somewhere." He paused, stroked her hand. "I hurt them when I ignored the plans they'd made for me. More when I married Adrianna. But it's past time for me to mend fences."

"I'd like that. Of course they might not like me any more than they liked her." For all Adrianna's faults, Shelly couldn't imagine that Kurt's parents wouldn't have been proud to see their son with such a beautiful woman. Especially since she came from old Atlanta money and high society.

Kurt bent and kissed the tip of her nose. "They can't help but fall in love with you."

When Shelly reached up to caress Kurt's cheek, the motion made her acutely aware of the fullness in her breasts. "Are the babies strong enough to nurse?" she asked.

"I don't know. You're sore, aren't you?" Very gently, he laid a hand on the lower curve of one breast. "You feel hot. No wonder you're sore. Where the hell is Brian?"

"Right here. Good morning to you, too." Brian came in, flipped open Shelly's chart, read a bit, and handed it to the resident who'd followed him into the room before giving Shelly a casual once-over.

"Nice flowers you've got already. By the way, you're looking good."

Shelly imagined she looked even more disheveled than Kurt, but that was the least of her concerns.

"I want to see my babies."

Brian took out a stethoscope and held it to her chest. "Okay. I'll see what I can do about getting you unhooked from most of these tubes, and then your husband can take you for a wheelchair ride. First, let me take a look."

Shelly tried not to wince when he checked the surgical dressing, but when he gently palpated her breast, she let out a yelp.

Brian turned to his resident. "Keith, write orders for a breast pump."

"Yes, sir."

He looked back at Shelly. "Unless you'd rather I give you something to dry up your milk. It may be a while before the babies are strong enough to nurse."

"No."

"All right. You can check with the babies' doctors. They'll probably want you to collect breast milk to feed them. Meanwhile, I'm going to order you some real food, and if you can eat it, you can lose the IV. The catheter can come out, as well."

"Isn't it a little soon for that?" Kurt asked.

Brian laughed. "Keith, meet Kurt Silverman. Best bone trauma man around. Unfortunately OB's a little out of his ballpark."

Kurt chuckled. "Are you telling me to butt out?"

"I'm telling you to forget you're a doctor while you're on my turf and play doting husband and daddy. Let me do my thing. I wouldn't stand over you and try to tell you how to repair my kid's broken leg or arm."

Kurt extended his hand across the bed, and Brian shook it. "Deal," he said. "You impressed the hell out of me yesterday, by the way."

"All in a day's work."

* * * * *

"Kurt, please hurry."

The time it took for the nurses to carry out Brian's orders must have seemed like forever to Shelly. It had been no picnic for him.

He laughed. "A wheelchair will only go so fast."

And the hospital's elevators seemed even slower than usual. Finally Kurt pushed her through the swinging door marked Neonatal Intensive Care.

Fifty-fifty. The neonatologist's odds resounded in his head.

He pushed Shelly's chair into a small room furnished with a padded rocker and two straight chairs, and buzzed for a nurse.

A resident and a nurse brought their babies. Compared with the last time Kurt saw them, they looked good. No machines and no monitors at the moment, though Kurt noticed EKG leads taped to his daughter's tiny body.

The nurse left. The resident lifted their squalling son and laid him in Shelly's arms, then sat in the second straight chair. "That little guy seemed hungry this morning. He may be strong enough to nurse a bit if you're up for giving it a try."

Shelly's smile was brighter than a ten-carat diamond as she held her son. And when the baby found her nipple and began to nurse, Kurt's fears began to subside.

He looked at his little girl, lying quietly in her isolette.

"If you want to hold her, Dr. Silverman, you can. We just fed her a few minutes ago."

Too choked up to talk, Kurt nodded. And he held his tiny daughter for a long time, keeping her warm against his chest. Finally he met the resident's gaze.

"How are they?"

"Amazingly strong, considering they're twins and premature. Your son's just an ounce short of four pounds, and your daughter weighs three pounds five ounces. Both of them have good lung development and strong reflexes.

"Barring any complications, you should be able to take the boy home in another two weeks. Your daughter will probably need to stay longer."

Barring complications. A doctor's caveat.

Kurt started sweating, because he knew enough to be aware of the many things that could go wrong, but not enough to make an educated guess as to the likelihood that some or all of those horrific events might actually happen.

"They're beautiful," Shelly said when they got back to her room.

Kurt put away his worries and took her hand. "Yes, they are. And so are you. I'm a lucky guy." And holding his daughter while watching her nurse their tiny son, tears in her dark green eyes, was as erotic a sight as he'd ever seen. He'd wanted to build a cocoon around them all, protect them all from harm.

She traced a circle on his palm with her thumb. "They're going to make it, Kurt. Just like you promised."

"I know. And I loved them the minute I saw them." The emotions that welled inside him made words come hard. But these words needed saying. "I love you, Shel. I need a kick in the ass for not realizing it until I thought I might lose you."

She squeezed his hand, looked at him with shining eyes. "Better late than never, my friend."

"Yeah."

When he bent and kissed her, he remembered the marriage vows he'd made by rote and silently repeated them — this time meaning every word.

"You're my life," he said when he raised his head.

"I love you, too." She grinned. "Now, let's name our babies so you can get back to your patients. You know, they need you, too, and I've monopolized your attention long enough."

They decided to name the babies Zachary and Sabrina, for his grandfather and Shelly's mom. When Jason called a few minutes later, Kurt handed the phone to Shelly.

"I'm glad he's enthusiastic about his brother and sister," she said when they'd hung up. "In a way, it's good Zach and Sabrina decided to come early, because now I should be able to do more than just lie around while he's here during the holidays."

Joy radiated from Shelly's eyes, caught Kurt up in love and filled him with hope for the family they'd share.

"We're all going to make it. Now and always," he said as he leaned over the bed to place a loving kiss on his wife's lips.

Epilogue

New Year's morning, Shelly stayed with Zach while Jason went with his dad to bring Sabrina home from the hospital. Dr. Blackstone and his wife had pulled in just as they drove away, and Jason figured the rest of his dad's office crew would be there by the time they got back. He was looking forward to shooting baskets with some of the older kids Shelly said would be at the party.

Now, though, he was busy watching his baby sister wriggle around in the car seat next to him.

"Wow. For being so little, she's got some kind of grip. And she just gave me a big grin." Jason tugged lightly, and Sabrina let go of his little finger.

Dad pulled into the garage, then turned and smiled. He seemed a lot more relaxed now than Jason recalled having ever seen him.

"Was I ever that small?" Jason watched Dad lift Sabrina out of the car seat, carry her upstairs, and lay her in the wicker bassinet next to Zach's.

Dad put an arm across Jason's shoulders. "Not quite. You were a big bruiser of a baby. Come on, let's go downstairs and help Shelly entertain our guests."

Dad and Dr. Blackstone stood to the side of the commotion and talked while Mrs. Blackstone helped Shelly put frosting on some bell-shaped cupcakes Jason could hardly wait to scarf down on.

"Go on outside. There are plenty of these for everybody," Shelly told him. "You can help the little kids break open those piñatas you and your dad hung up around the patio. They're getting a little antsy, and I don't want anybody falling into the pool."

Jason would be spending a lot more time here, now that the judge had listened to him and given Dad joint custody. Mom hadn't fought it very hard this time. Maybe that was because she was too busy planning her wedding to an older guy who seemed pretty cool himself, even though he didn't bake mouth-watering brownies like Shelly did.

Yeah, things were looking up. Like Shelly told him, Dad loved them all—and it wasn't the quantity as much as the quality of time they spent together that made them a happy family.

Jason had no doubt now that Dad loved him, not since Shelly told him a few days ago about the mutual favors they'd agreed to do for each other when they married.

He looked in through the kitchen window and saw Dad hug Shelly and steal a kiss. Instinctively he made the disgusted sounds almost-thirteen-year-old boys were supposed to make when they caught grownups doing something mushy.

But hey, it was killer, having his dad and Shelly so obviously crazy about each other. After all, he knew they were just as nuts over him and his baby brother and sister as they were for each other.

He turned to their guests and grinned. "Come on, kids, let's have at these piñatas. Gotta bring in the New Year right."

* * * * *

Long after the guests had gone home and Jason had zoned out in his room with his headphones and some new CDs, Kurt laid Zach in his crib and tucked a soft blue blanket around his sturdy little body. He'd been fussy tonight, as though unhappy about having to share his mom with little sis—even after he'd taken his late—night feeding.

Kurt knew how he felt. Watching Shelly nurse his babies only made him want her more—and tonight she'd made it clear she was tired of waiting, too.

The night light in the nursery cast her in shadow as she fed Sabrina, made her coppery hair and soft skin glow. Her lips slightly open and glistening wet from the kiss they'd shared earlier, she was the quintessential fertility goddess.

The siren who lured men to their ruin.

His siren had on the same peachy confection she'd worn on their wedding night, its lace top lowered to bare the ripe, full breasts that beckoned his hands and mouth but which now were bursting with milk to nourish their babies.

Her belly, not quite as flat as before, reminded him she'd taken his seed, nourished it, put herself in jeopardy to give birth to these two precious lives that were part of him and her.

His cock had never been so hard nor his balls so tight. He'd never experienced anything as erotic as the picture before his eyes.

Suddenly Sabrina's little mouth slackened and Shelly's elongated nipple slid free, rosy pink and pebbled against the brownish areola. When Shelly lifted the baby onto her shoulder, Kurt bent, cupped the satin orb and sucked the tip gently between his teeth.

Sweet. So sweet. When he circled her areola with his tongue, she rewarded him with another taste of the life-giving nectar.

"Sabrina's asleep. Want to put her in her bed?" Shelly asked, her voice siren-husky, mother-soft.

Kurt rose, lifted his little girl. How tiny, this miracle of life! he thought as he carried her to her crib next to Zach's, laid her in it, and arranged the coverlet.

Still tiny, Sabrina looked even more so in her father's muscular arms. But oh! What a rush to see them like this, her magnificently naked husband tucking in his swaddled baby girl, smoothing back the fine dark hair from her brow, and checking to be certain the infant monitor was working properly.

Primed while she'd watched Kurt and fed their babies, Shelly's need turned white-hot when she thought that now, for the first time in six long weeks, they could express the love they'd finally found with no restrictions.

He smiled at their babies, snug in their cribs. Then he turned to her and smiled, and she rose and went into his arms.

"We've finally got the babies to bed. Now I want to celebrate New Year's with my wife."

As though she weighed no more than little Sabrina, Kurt lifted Shelly and carried her to the bed, following her onto the downy featherbed.

His lean body, so hot and hard against her belly and breasts, the pulsing vein in his neck—the throbbing of his swollen cock against her mound—all mocked the deliberate, gentle pace he'd set with slow caresses, gentle nips at her earlobes. Light nibbling kisses circling her lips but never moving in to claim her mouth.

When she stroked his back and ass his muscles rippled like a jungle cat on the verge of springing for its prey. Yet he stayed the course, following his hands with his velvety tongue, his mouth with long, slender fingers.

"No more. It's been too long," she begged when the pressure got so intense she thought she'd die if he didn't give her some release. "Come inside me now."

"Tonight I'm going to show you just how much I love you," he murmured against her hair before slipping on a condom and settling between her outstretched legs. "I just don't want to risk you getting pregnant again — not yet."

Kurt loved her warmth, her wetness. The eager way she clutched his ass cheeks, her eager whimpers when he rubbed his cock head along her slippery slit. The way she dropped eager kisses along his jaw, his earlobe…a sensitive spot she'd found just above his collarbone.

Slowly, gently, he entered her. Her heat fed his, and when she lifted her hips and took him deeper than he'd have dared to go this first time, it was all he could do to keep from exploding.

But he wanted more. Wanted to savor the gift she gave him, show her the love he'd expressed these last week in words, in chaste touches, in every little act he'd come up with.

Tears sparkled in her deep-green eyes as she moved in tandem with his every measured thrust. Like diamonds on emeralds, sparkling crystal on pale, creamy cheeks. Her lips, glistening and slightly open, the corners turned up in a smile that bespoke joy, not pain.

How had he ever thought he didn't love her? Shelly was his life...his present and God willing his future.

"Kurt. Love. Make me come," she begged, her hips shifting restlessly under him, urging him to speed up the pace.

She didn't have to ask twice. "Oh, yeah," he growled when she took him deeper, clasped his cock inside her tight, wet pussy.

"Yesss. Oh, God. Don't stop!" Her inner muscles clenched him, held him, coaxed him to follow her to heaven.

He didn't need coaxing. The pressure mounted in his balls, robbed him of control. Mindlessly he plunged deep inside her. Once. Twice. On the third thrust he exploded, adding his triumphant shout to her ecstatic moans.

He was one lucky SOB to have proposed that he and Shelly do each other a mutual favor, because if he hadn't, he wouldn't have rediscovered love.

About the author:

Ann Jacobs welcomes mail from readers. You can write to her c/o Ellora's Cave Publishing at P.O. Box 787, Hudson, Ohio 44236-0787.

Also by ANN JACOBS:

- Awakenings
- Captured (anthology with Carroll Mavis-Raine)
- Colors of Magic
- Enchained (anthology with Jaid Black & Joey W. Hill)
- Firestorm
- He Calls Her Jasmine
- In His Own Defense
- Love Magic
- Love Slave
- Mystic Visions (anthology with Myra Nour & Sahara Kelly)

Why an electronic book?

We live in the Information Age—an exciting time in the history of human civilization in which technology rules supreme and continues to progress in leaps and bounds every minute of every hour of every day. For a multitude of reasons, more and more avid literary fans are opting to purchase e-books instead of paperbacks. The question to those not yet initiated to the world of electronic reading is simply: *why?*

1. *Price.* An electronic title at Ellora's Cave Publishing runs anywhere from 40-75% less than the cover price of the <u>exact same title</u> in paperback format. Why? Cold mathematics. It is less expensive to publish an e-book than it is to publish a paperback, so the savings are passed along to the consumer.

2. *Space.* Running out of room to house your paperback books? That is one worry you will never have with electronic novels. For a low one-time cost, you can purchase a handheld computer designed specifically for e-reading purposes. Many e-readers are larger than the average handheld, giving you plenty of screen room. Better yet, hundreds of titles can be stored within your new library—a single microchip. (Please note that Ellora's Cave does not endorse any specific brands. You can check our website at www.ellorascave.com for customer recommendations we make available to new consumers.)

3. *Mobility.* Because your new library now consists of only a microchip, your entire cache of books can be taken with you wherever you go.

4. *Personal preferences are accounted for.* Are the words you are currently reading too small? Too large? Too...**ANNOYING**? Paperback books cannot be modified according to personal preferences, but e-books can.

5. *Innovation.* The *way* you read a book is not the only advancement the Information Age has gifted the literary community with. There is also the factor of what you can read. Ellora's Cave Publishing will be introducing a new line of interactive titles that are available in e-book format only.

6. *Instant gratification.* Is it the middle of the night and all the bookstores are closed? Are you tired of waiting days—sometimes weeks—for online and offline bookstores to ship the novels you bought? Ellora's Cave Publishing sells instantaneous downloads 24 hours a day, 7 days a week, 365 days a year. Our e-book delivery system is 100% automated, meaning your order is filled as soon as you pay for it.

Those are a few of the top reasons why electronic novels are displacing paperbacks for many an avid reader. As always, Ellora's Cave Publishing welcomes your questions and comments. We invite you to email us at service@ellorascave.com or write to us directly at: P.O. Box 787, Hudson, Ohio 44236-0787.

Printed in the United States
25314LVS00001B/73-357